MINSTREL'S LEAP

When Verona Dean reads of the sudden
death of Sister Hyacinth, she travels to
Yorkshire to pay tribute to her friend's
memory. At *Minstrel's Leap* she hears of
the legend of Lady Eadgyth and her
troubadour lover, and meets the nuns of
St. Dorothy's. Gentle women, leading
dedicated lives — yet two have already
died, and a third is marked down as the
victim of a maniac who comes by night.
Verona sets out to discover the secret of
Minstrel's Leap, and is herself changed by
the happenings that take place there.

Books by Veronica Black
Published by The House of Ulverscroft:

A VOW OF SILENCE
VOW OF CHASTITY
MY NAME IS POLLY WINTER
VOW OF SANCTITY
MASTER OF MALCAREW
VOW OF PENANCE
A FOOTFALL IN THE MIST
VOW OF FIDELITY
VOW OF POVERTY
VOW OF ADORATION
GREENGIRL
VOW OF COMPASSION

VERONICA BLACK

◆

MINSTREL'S LEAP

Complete and Unabridged

ULVERSCROFT
Leicester

First published in Great Britain in 1973 by
Robert Hale Limited
London

First Large Print Edition
published 2000
by arrangement with
Robert Hale Limited
London

British Library CIP Data

Black, Veronica, *1935 –*
Minstrel's Leap.—Large print ed.—
Ulverscroft large print series: mystery
1. Detective and mystery stories
2. Large type books
I. Title
823.9'14 [F]

ISBN 0–7089–4263–6

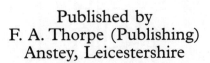

Published by
F. A. Thorpe (Publishing)
Anstey, Leicestershire
Set by Words & Graphics Ltd.
Anstey, Leicestershire
Printed and bound in Great Britain by
T. J. International Ltd., Padstow, Cornwall

This book is printed on acid-free paper

Author's Note

As far as I know the Order of the
Daughters of Compassion, mentioned in
this novel, has no foundation in fact; and
though I number many professed nuns
among my friends, none of them appears
under any guise in this purely fictional
story.

1

The day began like any other day, with a breakfast of tea, toast and marmalade, and the boiled egg that Mrs. Williams always put hopefully on the tray. She was of the opinion that one should begin the morning with a solid meal, and either could not, or would not, understand that I could exist quite happily until noon on a buttered roll and a cup of black coffee.

'Dry bread and coffee. Goes straight to your arteries, Miss Dean, and hardens them!' she prophesied darkly. 'Now you'd not be wanting iron arteries when you're scarcely into your twenties, would you?'

'I'd not be wanting a thirty-inch waist either,' I said dryly.

'Have *I* got a thirty-inch waist?' she demanded, twisting her spryly corseted figure about. 'Twenty-four inches, miss, for all that I've buried two!'

She was referring to husbands, not children, but her glance was maternal as it rested on me.

'You're as thin as a sparrow, miss, and I'm not surprised. Picking up all those

nasty, non-eating, Continental ways! Whatever would your poor, dear father say if he
could see you now?'

Because I didn't want to talk about my
father, I bent my head over the tray and
dutifully tapped the top of the egg.

'It's not as if you got yourself a decent
midday meal,' Mrs. Williams continued, in
the slightly flustered tone of one who knows
she has been tactless. 'Oh, you promise to eat,
but ten to one, when the hour strikes, you're
messing about with your easel and paints and
food's the last thing that crosses your mind!'

She meant to be kind, I know, and I knew
also that few landladies would take so much
trouble over a single young lady forced to
earn her own living. But, oh! how I longed for
her to be quiet and stop fussing and leave me
in peace.

I intended to walk down to the Embankment this morning and make some
preliminary sketches for a study of the river I
was planning. I saw it in my mind, flowing
brown with gleams of silver below the grey
walls. And perhaps, in the foreground, a dark
smudge of figure to point the loneliness.

My father would not have appreciated the
beauty in such a scene. For him, brilliance of
colour and swirling movement were the
keynotes of any painting. That was why we

had lived abroad for so much of the time, following the white hot sun through Spain and Italy while my father sought to capture that heat in the thick, sweeping strokes of paint that blazed angrily from all his canvasses.

'A painting must speak to you, girl, not whisper!' he had raged. 'Your sketches are timidly pretty, hinting and never stating.'

The trouble was that *his* pictures shouted. There was no peace in them, no restful corner where the eye could linger. They assaulted the senses, making one feel a trifle dizzy as one's eyes attempted to follow the spirals of red and gold and magenta.

He sold very few. On the Continent it had not mattered very much. We had lived cheaply there, sometimes camping out like gypsies, sometimes paying for our suppers by a lightning sketch of the landlord.

But in England matters were different. We had lived in England before, of course. My mother had died when I was eleven, and her death had released my father from the little Wiltshire village where we had had a small house. Released him from the bondage of his job as schoolmaster and the everlasting nagging of my mother's sharp tongue. He had given in his notice to the School Board, had sold the house, and with me trailing along at his side, had taken the first ship for Europe.

We had come back to England every summer after that; not to the village where I had spent my childhood, but to London. We had always stayed at Mrs. Williams's boarding house for two months in July and August.

When it rained my father stayed indoors, swearing he would never again set foot in such a waterlogged hell-hole, but when the sun shone we went out in the streets and wandered about, watching the flower-girls in Piccadilly, the costermongers and buskers, the organ-grinders with their red-coated monkeys. My father was happy then, but on the first day of September, we always packed our bags and set off again on our travels.

Last year I had returned to London alone. Last year I had — but I didn't want to think about that June of Eighteen Seventy-nine. I didn't want to think about my father as I had seen him last.

I concentrated instead on the congealing egg and the cooling toast. After breakfast, I would hurry down to the Embankment, and after lunch, I would put my sketching materials in my satchel and trudge off to the Misses Bloom. They were three young ladies to whom I gave drawing lessons once a week for five shillings an hour. They were all blonde, all charming, and all completely without talent.

I had acquired three other pupils during the last fifteen months and I had managed to sell two small canvasses. At best it was a meagre living. Had it not been for Mrs. Williams I would have gone hungry many a time.

The landlady, tiring of my silence, had gone into the back regions where I could hear her carrying on a lively altercation with the boy who delivered the fish.

'Haddock! Fresh haddock was what I ordered, not this bit of chewed-up yellow leather! However can I offer this to my guests? Why, they'll be insulted and I'll not be able to blame them!'

I smiled to myself, knowing that the other 'guests' consisted of two retired governesses who were conditioned into eating anything that was put before them, and a peppery Colonel who never touched fish under any circumstances.

'Three shillings for a bit of fish that looks as if it crawled up on the beach and surrendered!' Mrs. Williams exclaimed, returning with the offending purchase draped limply over a piece of newspaper.

As usual I was eating breakfast alone, the other occupants having taken their meal earlier, no doubt with many comments on the shockingly lazy habits of the younger generation.

'I'll have to poach it in milk, and hope it doesn't go off, I suppose,' she went on gloomily, slapping the fish into a tureen and eyeing it with misgiving. 'Are you going to be in for lunch?'

I nodded, sipping the dregs of my too milky tea.

'Well, don't forget to take an umbrella. It looks like rain.' Mrs. Williams glanced towards the overcast sky beyond the window and hurried out, raising her voice into a genteel shriek as she summoned the little maid-of-all-work. 'Kitty! *Kitty!* Will you put your skates on and come here at once!'

So there would be fish for lunch with pale, mashed potatoes and dark cabbage. There had been semolina shape for dessert the previous day. That meant plum tart to follow the fish. My soul ached for fat figs and ripe melons and chicken wings braised in cheap red wine.

Rain spattered the window-pane in a spiteful little gust. I would need my galoshes and ulster. I went over to the mirror above the chimney-piece to smooth down my hair. My face was framed between a box decorated with coloured shells and a twisted candlestick with 'A Present From Brighton' adorning its base.

My features were small and pale, too pale for a girl of twenty-three, and there were shadows under my eyes. I wore my hair in the way my father had liked it, centre-parted and drawn back into a heavy chignon. It was blue-black in colour and my eyes were grey. The black dress I wore with its narrow white collar made me look too prim, but at least it was neat and hard-wearing. I was forced to stretch my money to the utmost limits.

Quite suddenly, I was depressed by the thought of an endless succession of rainy mornings, fish lunches, and pupils who had no interest in art beyond the exact delineation of bunches of flowers stuck into china vases. Perhaps I had been mistaken in coming back to England. Perhaps I should have remained on the Continent, even without the protection of my father.

There was a rustling of skirts and Mrs. Williams hurried in, her sharp nose quivering with news. In one hand she clutched a piece of torn newspaper, and her voice shook a little.

'Miss Dean, oh, Miss Dean! I just laid eyes on this bit in the paper. It's here, what the fish was wrapped in. I saw the name just as I was looking through the obituary column. I do like having a little read of the obituaries, but seeing her name gave me ever such a nasty turn!'

She was pointing to an item in the grease-stained sheet. I went to her and read it at her elbow.

'Mayhew — Miss Helen Mayhew (Sister Hyacinth) aged 30. Suddenly, at St. Dorothy's Convent, Minstrel's Leap, Hepton, Yorkshire, on 19th September, 1880. R.I.P.'

Six summers fell away and I was a girl of seventeen again, exclaiming in horror over my friend's decision.

'Go into a convent! Helen, you can't possibly be serious. What in the world would you do there?'

'Work and pray, dear. Pray and work.'

Eyes twinkling, voice lilting into laughter, Helen had never been pretty, but she sparkled with life.

'You'll hate it, Helen. You know you will! Are you in love and have you been jilted?'

At seventeen, I could think of no other reason for entering a convent.

'You are a goose, Verona! I'm not in the least in love with any man, and if I were and had been jilted, why! I'd rush out and find another sweetheart!'

By the time we came back to London the following summer, Helen Mayhew had become Sister Hyacinth of the Daughters of Compassion. We had had a neat little card from her, written in a delicate, slanting hand that already set her apart. I had never answered that card. My main emotion had been one of selfish disappointment.

Helen had been my friend — the older sister I had never known, who was always at the boarding house when we returned each year. Helen had listened to the stories of our travels, advised sympathetically when I had defied my father and put up my hair, spent whole days with me when my father got an idea in his head for a painting and went off into a dream world, forgetting that he had a daughter.

For three summers Helen Mayhew had been my friend and then she had turned into Sister Hyacinth and I had never answered her card.

'Every Christmas she sent me a letter,' Mrs. Williams mourned. 'Only a few lines to tell me she was well and happy, and I'd send a few lines back.'

She had mentioned the letters before, had offered to show them to me, but I had refused.

'And now the poor soul is dead! I knew no good would ever come of shutting herself up! It's not natural, that's what it is! Oh dear, this has put me off for the whole morning. Is there a drop of tea left in the pot? I'm all of a quiver!'

Mrs. Williams sat down heavily and reached for a china-busted lady whose knitted skirts protected the round teapot. I sat down too and read the item again.

'It says 'suddenly',' I pointed out. 'I wonder what illness she had.'

I could almost see Mrs. Williams considering and discarding various sinister ailments. After a few minutes she said, 'It could have been an accident, I suppose, but I can't think what sort it could be.'

Neither could I, and we sat staring at each other for a few minutes. Then another thought struck me.

'Did Helen have any relatives? She told me once that she was an orphan.'

'She had an aunt over in Westmorland, I think, but she never spoke very much about her family.'

'She worked as a companion, didn't she?' Snatches of half-remembered conversations were coming back to me.

'Not actually a paid companion. She had a little money of her own and she was too independent to take a living-in post. She used to work at a Home for Decayed Gentle-women over at Streatham three days a week, and sometimes she took in a little sewing. Fine embroidery, nothing common or vulgar. She never worked in the summer though.'

'No, she placed herself at my disposal then.'

I had never thanked her for it, never done anything but take her friendship completely for granted and push her out of mind when she was no longer there.

'I can't make out what she was doing up in Yorkshire.' Mrs. Williams frowned over the newspaper. 'Her convent was in Norfolk. St. Dorothy's Convent. I had a note from her there last Christmas. She never mentioned anything about moving.'

'Perhaps she only just went to Yorkshire. I suppose nuns do get transferred from time to time?'

'I couldn't say, I'm sure,' Mrs. Williams, a staunch Episcopalian, said, and sipped her cooling tea primly. After a moment she said, surprisingly, 'Somebody ought to go up there.'

'For the funeral? But it says she died on the nineteenth. That was a week ago.'

'It just doesn't seem right,' she mused. 'Her dying like that, with no relatives or friends knowing about it, in a place nobody ever heard about.'

'Suddenly.'

And when I had spoken the word I felt chilly as if Mrs. Williams had poured the dregs of her tea down my back.

'Somebody ought to go up there,' she said, after a moment.

'Up to Yorkshire? But if Helen is dead, would there be any point in it?'

'Someone ought to make sure that everything has been done properly,' she insisted. 'If I'd known before this I might have tried to make the journey myself, but I really cannot see how it's to be managed, not by *me*, at all events.'

She gave me an arch little smile which I pretended not to notice.

'It's not that I couldn't afford the fare of course,' she went on guilelessly. 'Why, if there was anybody who'd make the trip on my behalf I'd gladly pay their expenses, train and board!'

'It would seem so odd, my just arriving without warning,' I said feebly.

'You're an artist, aren't you?' she countered. 'What's to prevent your staying in the village — what's its name? Hepton? — and taking a little sketching holiday?'

'What's to prevent my simply arriving at

the convent and telling them I'm a friend of Helen Mayhew's?'

Mrs Williams set down her cup, hitched up her skirt and leaned forward.

'I have a feeling about it,' she said solemnly.

I knew all about my landlady's feelings. They usually attacked her just after some catastrophe had been reported.

'I knew it. I had a 'feeling' when I looked at her,' had been her reaction to the news that Mrs. Atkins, from No. 17, had been knocked down by an omnibus.

'There! That's accounted for the 'feeling' I've had this past week,' summed up her response to the information that Amy Dolling had eloped with the grocer's assistant a few days before she was due to marry the grocer.

'I always go by my feelings, Miss Dean,' she said earnestly. 'And I have a very nasty feeling about Miss Mayhew's death — a very nasty feeling indeed!'

Her bony little face under the high cap she affected in the mornings should have made me smile at its anxious and triumphant foreboding, but I felt no impulse towards amusement.

'Tell you what, dear. We'll take a little peep at the tea-leaves,' she proposed. 'It's not a practice I'm addicted to normally, but there might be no harm in it; just this once.'

She said exactly the same thing at least twice a week to my certain knowledge. Some of my sense of humour returned as I obediently turned my cup upside down and swivelled it three times in an anti-clockwise direction. Mrs. Williams took it from me and gazed into its depths, pursing her small mouth critically.

'There's a gentleman here. A tall, dark gentleman,' she pronounced.

There was nothing very new about that. According to Mrs. Williams there were hundreds of tall, dark gentlemen sitting about in the bottoms of dirty cups.

'And a journey. I can see a train.'

'Going up to Yorkshire, I suppose?' I commented dryly.

'And a face looking out of a high pointed window.' She took no notice of my remark. 'Look! It's quite distinct!'

I looked but could see only a mass of sugar-drenched leaves adhering to the sides and base of the wet cup.

'Oh, my! Now this *is* interesting!' She had taken back the cup and was peering at it intently.

'What is it?'

'A gallows. A gallows with a figure hanging. It's a sign of death. Unnatural death.'

I looked at her in surprise for she had pushed the cup away from her and laced her trembling fingers together.

'You might be mistaken, Mrs. Williams,' I began.

'The leaves never lie,' she corrected firmly. 'It's very clear there. I've never seen it clearer. And I don't like it. I don't like it at all.'

It was foolish but my own hands were trembling too. I said swiftly, to lighten the moment, 'Perhaps the tall, dark gentleman will save me.'

'I'm not at all sure it was a good idea to think of going up to this Hepton place,' she said doubtfully. 'It's a long journey for a young lady to make.'

We were both aware that I had crossed the Channel alone, and that I often travelled about London by myself.

'It probably would be rather expensive,' I agreed blandly.

'Heavens! I'd not grudge the expense,' Mrs. Williams said soberly. 'I've a bit laid by, and there's nothing I'd rather spend some of it on than finding out what happened to Miss Mayhew.'

'She died,' I said.

It was odd how the two words killed her all over again. *Killed*? It was a strange word to float into my mind.

15

'Perhaps we could simply write to the convent and ask for details,' I suggested.

'They probably wouldn't tell us anything. After all nobody let me know about her death.'

'If she'd been transferred since Christmas they might not know your address,' I suggested.

Mrs. Williams tapped her teeth with a roughened forefinger.

'It would relieve my mind, Miss Dean,' she confessed after a moment. 'I simply don't like to leave it like this.'

Her eyes were anxious as they rested on the cup.

'I would enjoy visiting the north,' I said cheerfully. 'I could pay back any money you spent on my account.'

She waved aside the idea of repayment.

'Would it be possible for you to leave fairly soon? What about your pupils, the young ladies you teach? Will their mamma give you leave of absence?'

From their progress under my tuition, I was fairly certain that their mamma would be only too pleased to give me a permanent leave of absence.

'I'm sure of it,' I said brightly. 'I'll see her this afternoon and tell her I'm going to take a holiday with some friends of mine. There'll be a train tomorrow, I suppose?'

'There are plenty going up to the north. I'll get Kitty to run down to the station and make enquiries. Are you sure about this, Miss Dean? Are you sure that you want to go?'

I was not sure at all, but it would at least be a change from rainy mornings and fish lunches. Something deeper than selfishness moved within me. This was something I could do for the young woman who had once been my friend.

'I wish I had written to her,' I said. 'I wish I hadn't lost touch with her so completely.'

The truth was that I had forgotten her. I had wiped her out of my mind because she had done something that seemed, in my immature mind, to constitute a betrayal.

'I'm not at all sure that I'm doing the right thing,' Mrs. Williams worried, pushing back her chair as she rose. 'Now that your father is dead I feel responsible for you.'

'I'll be fine,' I assured her.

'Well, you may meet the dark gentleman up in Hepton,' she said. 'A young lady ought to be wed.'

'Not *this* young lady!' I said sharply.

'Ah, you'll feel differently when you meet Mr. Right,' she said, shaking her finger at me.

I felt my mouth grow pinched and tight but I forced a smile to it as she began to clear away the dishes. Now and then she stopped to shake her head and exclaim over 'poor, dear Miss Mayhew'.

But Miss Mayhew, my friend Helen, had gone away six years before, and turned into Sister Hyacinth whom I didn't know, and to whom I had never written. I wondered what she would have said if I had been able to tell her about Pierre, and my father, and if her knowing would have made any difference?

I decided it was useless to speculate. It was probably more than useless to go up to Yorkshire on the strength of my landlady's 'feelings', but it would serve to break the monotony of my existence, to assuage my sense of guilt and my curiosity.

2

I was eager to be gone once I had made up my mind to it. My father and I had seldom planned our route. We had travelled simply where the fancy took us, packing and moving sometimes at an hour's notice. When we found cheap lodgings and a congenial atmosphere we would stay sometimes for two or three months.

For Mrs. Williams, however, a journey was a rare event to be pondered over and planned down to the last detail. She was still uncertain as to the wisdom of urging me to go, but shy of withdrawing her offer of financial assistance lest she be suspected of meanness.

As for me, I had long since forgotten any false pride my mother might have instilled in me. I gratefully accepted the ticket to York, and the ten sovereigns my landlady decided I might need for expenses.

'And your room will be kept for you while you're away, Miss Dean. You needn't fear that I'll put a stranger in your bed the moment your back is turned. I just want this matter cleared up for my own peace of mind.'

I believe she was genuinely concerned over

Helen's death, but I think she was moved also by an innocent craving for sensation. Mrs. Williams had a penchant for yellow-backed novels and for the more lurid of the newspapers. Disappointment would be mingled with her relief when I discovered that Helen had died quite naturally with no attendant mystery.

We let the weekend elapse before I began the journey. It took a longer time than I had expected to convince my pupils that I needed a leave of absence, but the invention of a sick friend at length mollified even Mrs. Bloom. By Monday my small trunk was corded, my money and my ticket were in my purse, and Mrs. Williams was giving me a spate of advice as we stood on the crowded platform.

'Now don't forget to write and let me have all the news. I won't expect to see you back in under a month, mind! You try and get some colour in your cheeks, now. A bit of a change will do you a power of good. Here's the train! Have you got those sandwiches I made? There's a nice corner seat here for you.'

My last view of her was through the plate-glass window of the compartment as she bobbed up and down, shaking her umbrella and holding her hat firmly on her head.

As the train pulled out and smoke

obscured her wiry little frame, I was quite startled by the depression that swept over me. Her fussing irritated me, but she was the only real friend I had, the only person who cared what happened to me. I opened my magazine with an air of determination and settled down to read it, though the words *Minstrel's Leap* blurred together over the essay on garden-party etiquette.

'It is advisable in very warm weather to provide water-sprinklers for the — '

Minstrel's Leap. Was it the name of the district where the convent was situated or the name of a house?

'Small nosegays might be offered to the ladies — '

And who was the Minstrel, and where had he leapt?

It was quite useless to concentrate. With a mental apology to the author of the essay I closed the magazine, and stared out at the dreary suburban landscape that slid past as we rattled north.

After a while I ate my sandwiches and then, in an effort to take my mind off unknown minstrels, began to sketch my fellow passengers in the pad I always carried within my satchel.

I had none of my father's exuberant talent but I could catch a likeness in a few strokes. I smiled to myself, as I saw the gleam of greed emerge in the stolid features of the elderly gentleman who sat dozing in the further corner.

Next to him sat a thin lady who held herself very erect as if she were afraid somebody might attempt to speak to her. I drew her in profile, giving her long nose a faintly offended air.

The sailor-suited child who bobbed up and down next to his plump mother on the opposite seat wouldn't keep still long enough for me to do more than make a very hasty little cameo.

The gentleman who had got in at the last station was more rewarding material. He was dark and sallow-complexioned with a coat that had something foreign about it, though whether this was revealed in its cut or in the slightly too wide velvet lapels I couldn't decide.

He was in his mid-thirties at a guess, and wore a narrow moustache that added to his faintly rakish air. I would have liked to draw him with his eyes open, but he had leaned back and was apparently sleeping.

I shaded my drawing carefully, trying to bring out the contrast between his clear-cut features and the slightly flamboyant suit. His hands were coarse, the fingers thick and reddened, the wrist jutting from his deep cuffs curiously powerful for a man of such slender build.

He opened his eyes suddenly, so suddenly that I jumped a little. Then, aware of my gaze, a faint amusement lighted his austere face, the somewhat patronising amusement of a man who knows himself to be attractive.

I flushed and glanced down at my pad before closing it. The sketch was not a good one. I had exaggerated the coarseness of the hands and the closed eyes lent a deceptive indolence to the face. I would touch it up later, remember that his open eyes were pale and bright, his mouth looser than I had made it.

He was still staring at me. For a moment I was afraid he had seen what I was doing. If so he would have had a right to object. To sketch somebody without permission is to violate their privacy, to catch them in an unguarded, secret moment. Yet I could not help studying people, reducing them to black lines and curves on a white background.

When my father and I had travelled together he had always brought out crayons and block quite openly, and within a few minutes he would have established himself as a friend, chatting to the men in a mixture of English and abominable French, flattering the women, making the children laugh with his songs and the faces he pulled as his crayons swirled across the paper.

That was how we had met Pierre. I closed my eyes and concentrated upon blackness, upon the noise of the engine, upon anything that would not remind me of Pierre. I had succeeded in forcing him out of my mind for months at a time, but there were still moments when he leapt back into my thoughts.

It was mid-afternoon when we reached York. The pale-eyed man had evidently lost interest in me, for he wrenched open the carriage door and hurried up the platform without glancing again in my direction.

I lifted down my own luggage and decided to buy a cup of tea, and a light meal in the small restaurant, close by the booking-office. It might be some time yet before I reached my destination, and it was hours since I had eaten the sandwiches.

The café was half-empty and sparsely furnished, but it was clean and the little waitress who served me strong tea and poached eggs had a round, cheerful face. While she was serving me I enquired whether it would be possible to get a train to Hepton.

'Hepton? That's a little place up Helmsley

way, miss. The line doesn't go right up there yet.'

'How far does it go?'

'Well, you could get the local train to Helmsley,' she suggested. 'There'll be cabs for hire there. I'm sorry I can't help you more, but one of the porters might tell you.'

I thanked her and finished my meal. When she returned with the bill she volunteered, 'There's a Helmsley train due out in ten minutes, miss. Goes straight there with no changes. You can buy a ticket at the booking-office.'

'Thank you very much.'

I added a tip to the money on the plate and felt my spirits lift. It seemed that my journey was being made smooth for me by the good nature of strangers. I hoped that it was a good omen.

The local train was packed with an assortment of passengers. Most of them seemed to know one another and there was a constant hubbub of conversation. I was fascinated by the speech with its broad vowels and laconic construction of grammar. The waitress in the café had been a 'city' girl, I guessed, and her accent had only flavoured her voice.

Some of these folks, crammed together with baskets on their knees, spoke in so distorted a fashion that it was only by deliberately attuning my ear that I was able to follow the sense of what they said. Most of it seemed to be about the harvest and the price of various commodities, but I pricked up my ears when the word 'Hepton' fell upon them.

'Excuse me, but I heard you mention Hepton.'

I had broken in too eagerly for there was an immediate silence as every head in the compartment swivelled towards me.

'I am travelling to Hepton myself,' I said. 'I wondered how far it was from Helmsley.'

'Not too long a step,' a man in the corner answered briefly.

'I was told I might get a cab at Helmsley,' I said awkwardly.

'Aye, if tha' hast brass to burn!' a woman said shrilly.

'I have a heavy case to carry,' I said, a trifle nettled at her tone.

'Tha' canst hire a cab at station.'

The speaker was a florid individual with a not ill-natured face.

'I was bound for *Minstrel's Leap*,' I began, wondering why I was bothering to explain anything to these unfriendly people.

'*Minstrel's Leap* is outside Hepton,' said the man in the corner. He had a narrow foxy face and gave the impression of having bred greyhounds.

'Tha'd do best to get off at t'level crossing,' said the florid gentleman. 'It's no more than a step across t'field then.'

It sounded better than the roundabout route through Helmsley. Certainly I had no desire to spend money on unnecessary cabs, and the day was wearing on faster than I had realized.

'It will be possible to get a room there, will it?' I enquired.

'There's a guest-house,' the shrill-voiced woman volunteered.

I smiled and they began to talk amongst themselves again. They had evidently summed me up and dismissed me as a stranger, a foreigner for whom they felt no particular liking. I began to fear that the friendliness of the girl in the café had been an exception to the general code of conduct in these parts.

'We'll be at t'level crossing in a minute,' said the foxy-faced man. 'Tha can give thy ticket to the man on t'gates. He'll send it down to clerk at Helmsley.'

'Up. Isn't Helmsley north of York?' I ventured.

'Aye, *up*, if tha's a mind t'be faddy!' the woman said scornfully.

Rebuked, I held my tongue, waiting eagerly for the train to slow down so that I could shake myself free of my uncongenial companions.

It afforded me a certain wry amusement to watch the alacrity with which, as the train drew to a standstill, the florid gentleman helped me down from the high step and handed out my trunk to me. Obviously they preferred to keep the compartment to themselves, without the intrusion of a stranger to limit their gossip.

I made my way through the gap in the white fence and gave my ticket to the man in the blue smock and peaked cap. He peered at it doubtfully and then squinted at me.

'This ticket's for Helmsley,' he said at last.

'I know, but I'm going to *Minstrel's Leap*. They told me on the train that I could get down here, and take a short cut across the field.'

'Aye, but it's a fair way.'

'They said it was just a step,' I protested.

'A step of a mile or more,' he said, looking sourly amused. 'Tha' mun go across t'field towards that clump of trees. Tha'll see a footpath.'

He pointed towards the wavering track cutting across the grass.

'Reckon t'folk on train were having a

laugh,' he continued, and shambled off to a hut a few yards away.

I gazed in exasperation at the now empty track, and wondered if the 'folk' were still enjoying the joke at my expense. It was obviously useless to run after the man in the smock and demand help. It was equally futile to stand at the fence gazing helplessly at my trunk.

Suppressing an unladylike expression my father had been in the habit of using, I bent and picked up the corded luggage, shifted my satchel to my other hand, and took the path that had been indicated to me. It was fortunate that day was crisp and sunny with no sign of the rain that had lashed the capital during the weekend.

Long before I had reached the trees, my trunk seemed to have acquired the weight of lead and my arms ached fiercely. I put my burden down on the path and flexed my hands as I stared round. The field was not only large but sloped uphill, and I had traversed only a small corner of it. To my left the sun was already dipping lower in the sky and a faint breeze ruffled the black ribbon on my hat.

I heard above the sighing of the grass a cheerful whistling and swung round to face the man who walked behind me. A tall man in shirt sleeves and breeches with a scythe over his shoulder, he was sauntering from the direction of the level-crossing. I realized, with a spurt of indignation, that he must have been following me for some considerable time and had only just chosen to make his presence known.

'If you're going to *Minstrel's Leap*, perhaps you would be kind enough to carry my bag,' I said sharply.

'Likely I might at that!' he agreed, grinning in an impudent fashion but making no effort to pick up the trunk. He was in his late twenties, I guessed, and attractive in a lively, nut-brown way.

'I can make it worth your while,' I said, too weary to be ashamed of the coaxing note that had come into my voice. 'I am a stranger here from London, and I got off the train at the level crossing.'

'Aye, you were seen.'

He looked and sounded amused, because, I thought irritably, he had been listening to my conversation from within the hut.

'Well, will you help me?'

'Reckon so,' he observed in the flat accents I had heard on the train. 'What will tha gie me?'

'A shilling,' I said recklessly.

The young man pushed back the black hair

dangling into his eyes and held out a grubby calloused palm.

'I'll tak' t'brass now,' he said.

Flushing with anger and embarrassment, I dug into my reticule and brought out a coin. He took it, bit it thoughtfully, and shoved it into the pocket of his stained breeches.

He picked up my trunk as easily as if it were a paper-bag and pushed ahead of me on the narrow path, leaving me to follow as best I could. I followed resentfully, hoping that I was not destined to encounter any more practical jokers or yokels.

The path curved sharply towards the trees and then veered downhill past them. Below, on the green plateau beyond the crest, I saw for the first time a large E-shaped building, the middle stroke of the letter missing and the two wings of the house stretching back from the main façade. It was built of grey stone, but lichen covered the walls so that it blended not unpleasantly into the surrounding grass.

'*Minstrel's Leap?*'

'Aye. It's a convent now. St. Dorothy, or some such. Mind tha doesna rick thy ankle. Going's rough.'

His warning was timely for the path was steeper here, and there were tufts of grass to tumble the unwary.

I followed cautiously until we were on level ground again. The grass swept up to the front of the house, unimpeded by hedge or flower bed, but a short flight of steps led up to the arched oaken door.

My companion dumped my trunk on the lowest step, and nodded towards a bell suspended at the side of the door.

'If tha pulls, summat might answer.'

He sketched a jerky bow, hoisted up the scythe and went whistling round the side of the house.

So *Minstrel's Leap* was a dwelling place, not a huddle of houses as I had imagined. Obviously that had been its original name, although now a neatly painted black and white board above the arch informed the visitor that this was St. Dorothy's Convent.

The house was large, but beautifully proportioned with six stained glass windows on each side of the main door. The rich jewel shades of the glass were magnificent, but rendered the windows completely opaque. To left and right of the central rectangle there was a double row of windows, not of stained glass but frosted in the lower panes.

I stood back to admire the gleams and shafts of light that glittered and shimmered from amid the quiet, lichen-covered stone. From where I stood the back-sweeping wings of the house were not visible, and the place had a Georgian simplicity of line.

This house had been built with loving care and added to only with the greatest tact. There were no cupolas here, no towers or battlements, only a high sloping roof with a wide central chimney, only a harmony of stone, slate and glass perfectly proportioned.

The foundations were probably old; the present building dated back, I imagined, to the reign of Elizabeth. Some great landowner must have raised this edifice as a monument to his own prosperity and as a home for his descendants. I imagined the portly figure riding over his acres and his wife with a brood of children at her skirts.

Somebody was studying me as intently as I was studying the house. I could sense eyes looking at me in the silence, and for an instant my heart thudded uncomfortably. For the first time I was aware of the isolation of this place. And of the quietness. Nothing seemed to move or stir behind the moss-clad walls, and there was no sign of the whistling man.

I stepped back and scanned the windows carefully. The feeling that one is being spied upon is not a pleasant one, and I could feel my temper beginning to rise. My eyes narrowed as I shaded them with my hand and peered up to one of the higher windows at the extreme right of the building. The lower panes of the glass were frosted, but in the clear space at the top a face was framed.

A girl was staring down at me with such intensity that her regard had drawn my own eyes. I saw her quite clearly behind the glass and my first reaction was pure pleasure at the loveliness of that heart-shaped face framed in long red hair that flowed down over shoulders draped in some dull golden stuff. This was a face I would love to paint, framed in the pointed arch.

Mrs. Williams had seen a face looking out from a pointed arch in the teacup. It was a coincidence, of course. But she had seen a tall, dark gentleman too. And a gallows. I remembered that, and then wished I had not remembered.

The girl was still gazing at me. I raised my hand in tentative greeting and to my surprise she brought her own hands together, joining them palm to palm, in the age-old gesture of pleading.

I frowned, shaking my head in bewilderment. The face at the high window became anguished and the fingers twined together and then were wrung over and over. I went on shaking my head and shrugging in a vain attempt to make her understand that

I could do nothing.

From the top of the steps a voice said, coolly pleasant,

'Good afternoon, Miss Dean. I understand that you walked up from the level-crossing. A pleasant walk, but a tiring one, don't you think? Do please come in.'

The speaker was a tall, slim nun, clad in the conventional black and white habit and veil of the religious. A gold crucifix gleamed at her waist and her bearing was one of such calm authority that I had meekly picked up my trunk and followed her within the newly opened door before I had realized it.

3

I stepped into an enormous, stone-flagged hall with a gallery running along the inner wall. Above, were more stained glass windows which cast lozenges of colour over the stone and age-blackened wood of the stairs spiralling up to the gallery.

The nun turned to the left and stood aside as she motioned me through an open door into a large, austerely furnished room.

'Do please sit down,' she said cordially, and waited until I had chosen a high-backed chair pulled up to the desk.

I couldn't help wondering how many of her nuns had been scolded here, for it was evident she was the Prioress. There was dignity in every line of her spare frame, and her voice held the poise of experience and breeding.

'Simon informed me that a young lady called Dean was about to ring for admittance. I decided to greet you myself. I am Mother Catherine.'

So the uncouth man with the scythe had read my name from the label on my trunk.

'I have had no word from Reverend

Mother General to expect a new postulate, but I assume you have a letter of recommendation from your parish priest?'

As the words registered my mouth opened in embarrassed horror. She had obviously mistaken me for a prospective member of the Order.

'Is there something wrong, my child?' she enquired.

'I'm afraid there's been a mistake,' I stammered. 'I'm not a — . I haven't come here to be a nun!'

My voice squeaked slightly, and a faint amusement lit her calm eyes.

'We seem to have begun with a complete misunderstanding,' she said. 'Perhaps we had better begin all over again. You *are* Miss Dean?'

'Miss Verona Dean,' I nodded. 'I hoped that I might obtain a room in the guest house. There *is* a guest house here?'

I was afraid momentarily that the practical jokers on the train had misled me on this point too.

'Yes, indeed. The west wing has been converted into a suite of guest rooms,' she assured me. 'It was stupid of me not to realize that you might be a visitor.'

But visitors would seldom arrive on foot clad in serviceable black. I could hardly blame her for imagining me to be a recruit for the religious life.

'The guest house is not paying well,' Mother Catherine said. 'We hoped that people who were in need of rest and quiet might come here, but the house is in too isolated a position, I fear. It may even become necessary to — advertise.'

Her voice dropped a trifle as she contemplated the dismal prospect. Then it brightened slightly.

'We have a very comfortable place here, but I'm afraid you will be the solitary guest which will at least ensure you individual attention. Only this is a very quiet spot for a young lady — '

She paused again, eyeing me doubtfully.

Now was the moment for me to spin the tale about the sketching holiday, but those candid eyes and that pale face repelled falsehood.

'I'm a friend — was a friend of Helen Mayhew — of Sister Hyacinth,' I blurted.

A thin white hand rose and fell in the sign of the cross. Then Mother Catherine leaned forward slightly.

'I had no idea that Sister Hyacinth had any friends in the world,' she said. 'I am so sorry that you come here on such a sad errand. She had been with us for only three weeks, you know, but it was clear she was destined to be an asset to the Community.'

'I'm not a close friend. I used to know her several years ago, before she became a nun. We lost touch after that. I have lived abroad for most of my life.'

'May I ask how you heard about Sister Hyacinth's death?' Mother Catherine enquired.

'In the obituary column.'

'Of *The Times*? Ah, yes, I did send a notice to that newspaper and asked that it be inserted in the London editions. I thought it might be advisable in case there could be a distant relative somewhere. There was, I believe, an aunt but we don't have her present address.'

'Her convent — I thought it was in Norfolk.'

'We have four convents in this country,' she explained. 'In Norfolk, Devon and on the borders of Shropshire. This is the latest foundation. We have been here ourselves for little more than a year. You were puzzled by the similar names, I daresay. All our convents are under the protection of St. Dorothy. This was a private house until very recently.'

'It's very beautiful.'

'This part is very early Tudor. The wings are late Elizabethan.'

She broke off and gave me a kindly, shrewd glance.

'You may decide not to stay,' she said, 'but it's too late for you to retrace your footsteps today. May I suggest that you stay overnight at least? We have supper at six if you would be kind enough to join us. Afterwards one of the Sisters will take you to the guest house. Now if you will excuse me for half an hour, I must go to Prayers. There is a small washroom here where you may freshen up. I will take you over to the refectory when I return.'

She rose, indicating an inner door, and went out with a smiling nod.

There was cold water, soap and towel in the little stone-walled room. I used them and tidied my hair as well as I could without the aid of a mirror. Back in the larger room I resisted the temptation to explore and sat down, hearing from somewhere in the building the ringing of a bell.

Despite myself I began imperceptibly to relax. The simplicity of stone walls and floor, the half-frosted windows, the few pieces of dark furniture induced tranquillity of mind.

It was very cool, though I noticed a fire laid ready in the grate and wondered if I might light it. I had the impression that such action on my part might be deemed impertinent however and so refrained.

Precisely on the half-hour as my watch indicated, Mother Catherine returned.

'If you will come with me, we will go over for supper now,' she said. 'After tonight, if you intend to stay, your meals will be served to you in the guest house.'

'You have not mentioned your terms,' I said awkwardly.

Her eyes flickered over me briefly as she assessed my financial situation.

'Would thirty shillings a week be too expensive?' she queried.

That meant I could safely take the room for at least a month.

'Thirty shillings would suit me very well.'

'Good. When you have seen the guest house we can discuss the matter further.'

She gave her little, efficient nod and led the way out into the hall.

As we crossed it I was struck again by the silence. It was hard to imagine that a group of women lived and worked here. The nun's shoes made no noise on the flag-stones as she glided past the high gallery to a door on the right.

We entered a small lobby with a door opposite and a door on the left. Mother Catherine entered the left-hand door.

'This is the east wing where we have our quarters. The room where you waited was the visitors' parlour. My own office and cell is above it.'

We passed through two large square panelled rooms into a third apartment. Here in the centre of the room was a long table with a bench down each side of it and a carved chair at head and foot.

Two rows of black-garbed women stood with bent heads and folded hands. The nun who stood behind the chair at the foot of the table turned as we entered and bowed slightly.

'Good evening, my daughters. We have a visitor to share our supper this evening. Miss Verona Dean will be spending the night in the guest house, and may be staying for a longer time.'

Mother Catherine's clear voice stirred a faint ripple among the waiting figures. She nodded to the tall nun who had bowed to us.

'Mother Marie is our Mistress of Novices,' she said pleasantly.

The nun bowed again silently, her deep-set eyes glowing in a strong, plain face. The nuns at one side of the table had moved up and another came through an inner door with an extra plate and cutlery.

I took my place shyly and Mother Catherine went to the chair at the head of the table where she intoned a short, Latin grace.

There was a series of rustles as the nuns seated themselves and unfolded large white napkins.

One of them, instead of eating, went over to a lectern in the corner of the room and opening a large book on it began to read aloud a portion of the Gospels, while the nun who had brought the extra plate began to move back and forth between the refectory and what was evidently the kitchen, with dishes of food.

The meal was good, a savoury concoction of crisp sausages with baked potatoes and onions. There was no talking, only the faint rattling of knives and forks, and the steady voice of the reader. I kept my eyes fixed on my plate and tried not to chew too audibly. The main course was succeeded by a baked apple sponge, wonderfully light and succulent.

At the conclusion of the meal, napkins were folded, the nuns rose, and Mother Catherine said another Latin prayer. Her tone warmed slightly as she glanced down the table towards me.

'We have our evening recreation now, Miss Dean. Perhaps you would be good enough to join us before you go over to the guest house? Sister Felicity, will you prepare the guest room before you come to recreation?'

A nun at the other end of the table inclined her head as the Prioress left her place. We followed her decorously into the nearer of the big-panelled rooms. There were high-backed chairs lining the walls and a pianoforte in one corner.

The Prioress, seeing my glance, said cordially, 'We are very fond of music here. Sister Bridget plays beautifully.'

A round-cheeked nun with bright blue eyes said, modestly, 'Ah, it's just the natural Irish genius in me coming out.'

'Sister Bridget swims home once a year to kiss the Blarney Stone,' said a fair-skinned, freckled nun.

'Mother Marie, may I leave it to you to introduce our Sisters? I have some business to attend.'

The Prioress beckoned the Novice Mistress, and withdrew.

'Well, now, Miss Dean, let me see if I can sort them out for you.'

The tall nun had a dry, crackling voice with a hint of humour somewhere at the bottom of it.

'Our self-confessed musical prodigy is Sister Bridget. This is Sister Perpetua.' She indicated the freckled girl. 'Sister Marguerite. Sister Damian. Sister Joan. Sister Felicity has gone over to the guest house. Sister Paul and

Sister Elizabeth are having their supper now.'

That would be the one who had read aloud and the one who had served the meal. The one who served had been tiny and plump; the reader bespectacled, with a grey veil instead of a black one.

Mother Marie indicated another clad in the same fashion.

'This is Sister Anne, the newer of our two novices.'

'You will never be able to remember us,' said the one called Sister Marguerite.

I smiled inwardly. Already my trained artist's eye was picking out the small differences in the features beneath the white coifs. When I had learned to distinguish their voices, I might be in a position to recognize them as individuals.

'We were beginning to despair of ever having a visitor,' Sister Bridget said merrily. 'Sister Felicity will be pleased. She used to be a nurse, and she enjoys fussing over folk.'

'I'm not here as a convalescent,' I told her. 'I was a friend of Sister Hyacinth's. I came up after reading of her death in the newspaper.'

'Ah, God rest the poor Sister!' The bright blue eyes softened. 'It was a sad loss to us all.'

'Sister Hyacinth was with us for only three weeks, but she settled down so happily,' said Sister Damian.

I had noticed her in particular for she was extremely lovely with enormous dark eyes and the sort of wild-rose complexion that most women spend a fortune in trying to acquire.

'May I ask how long you had known her?' Mother Marie enquired.

'My father and I used to stay at the same boarding house in London every summer,' I explained. 'I'm afraid I lost touch with her completely in recent years, but then I read about her death, and decided to travel up.'

'You will find that everything has been done correctly,' said Sister Joan, as if I had voiced a criticism.

'Father Justin preached a beautiful sermon.' Sister Bridget sounded moistly sentimental.

'As yet we have no resident chaplain, but Father Justin comes over from Hepton once a week to hear confessions and offer Mass,' said Sister Damian.

Her voice was as lovely as her face, being rich and warm. It was a pleasure to listen to her as well as look at her.

'Mother Catherine said that you hadn't been here in this convent for very long.'

'Just over a year,' said Mother Marie. 'We had a small house on the outskirts of York. A very pretty little building with an orchard behind.'

'We had been there for two years, ever since it was decided to establish a foundation in Yorkshire,' Sister Joan said in a less accusing tone.

'And then, due to mischance, we left York and were fortunate enough to find this beautiful house.'

Sister Marguerite had a sweet, fluting voice like a bird. She looked rather like a bird too, with tiny, claw hands and a sharp little nose like a beak.

'Is this your first visit to this part of the world?' Mother Marie asked.

'Yes, indeed.'

Under her amused gaze at my resentful tone I found myself telling them about the people in the train. Retailing the story made it seem funnier than it had been when I was trudging through the field.

'The local people do have an original way of welcoming strangers,' Mother Marie commented. 'They think it's amusing to set them at some disadvantage in order to discover their reactions.'

'In other parts of the world they shoot partridges and ducks for amusement,' I said.

The remark was meant to be sour, but the semi-circle of nuns rippled with laughter.

'They are the kindest people one could hope to meet once you get to know them better,' Mother Marie assured me. 'Most of them have been quite helpful since we moved in. I wish we could recruit more local girls as novices, however. Sister Paul is from Derbyshire; and Sister Anne is from Cornwall.'

She spoke a trifle wistfully. I had the impression that there was a good deal of the missionary spirit in this tall woman with the deep-set eyes and the dry, harsh voice. I could imagine her as the Prioress of a large and thriving Community.

'Have you travelled very far, Miss Dean?' Sister Perpetua asked.

'I came up from London.'

'Such a long way to travel!' Sister Marguerite twittered. 'Of course, young ladies do take long journeys these days. When I was a young girl, we never went anywhere unchaperoned, but times change.'

She sounded gently regretful.

'Miss Dean, do you play the pianoforte?' asked Sister Damian.

'Only a little. I was hoping that Sister Bridget might play.'

I glanced towards the rosy-cheeked Irish nun who immediately blushed even more redly.

'Do play, Sister,' the Mistress of Novices

urged. 'Come and sit down, Miss Dean. You will enjoy this, I assure you.'

The performance was indeed excellent. I am no judge of musical competence but it was evident that Sister Bridget had a lightness and a warmth of interpretation that would have earned considerable acclaim in the wider world. But though I listened with pleasure, part of my attention was fixed upon the nuns themselves.

I had drawn my chair back slightly and so had an excellent view of the faces framed in the coifs and veils. Mother Marie was an elderly woman, as were Sister Marguerite and Sister Joan. I had had the impression that Sister Felicity, who had not yet come back, was middle-aged. Sister Elizabeth, who now joined us with Sister Paul at her side, was somewhere in her thirties, I supposed. The two novices, Sister Anne, Sister Damian — they were still in their twenties. The girl I had seen wringing her hands at the upper window could not have been more than seventeen. And she had worn a robe of gold over which her pale red hair had streamed. These women hid their hair under tight head-dresses and their robes were black.

Applauding as Sister Bridget lifted her hands from the keys, I said, 'Am I truly the only guest? Are there no others here?'

'I wish there were. Such great schemes for the guest house were planned, but they all came to nothing,' Sister Perpetua regretted.

I was framing another query as Sister Felicity returned.

'The guest house is ready, Miss Dean, if you'd like to come over with me now to see your room. Then I can bring you down to Mother Catherine again,' she offered.

'Faith, and I'd hardly started the recital!' Sister Bridget cried. 'But we'll see you again at recreation, Miss Dean?'

'I shall make a point of joining you again if I may,' I said promptly.

These were the women with whom Helen Mayhew had spent the last three weeks of her life. I wanted to know them better, to spend more time in this beautiful old house. Somewhere in the building was a girl with long red hair and a golden dress. I wanted to see her again, to discover the reason for her anguished look.

I smiled my good nights to the Sisters, and followed Sister Felicity out into the great hall again. The light was fading fast to remind us that it was the latter end of September and my shoes rang hollow on the flagstones.

The nun glided silently as the Prioress had done. I wondered if they were trained to walk in this fashion or if they wore specially soled footwear to cut down unnecessary noise.

Sister Felicity had paused and glanced up towards the high gallery on our right. The stairs twisting up to it were blurred in the dimness and the windows above glowed dull blue and gold and red as they reflected the dying daylight. The unpleasant thought that somebody could stand on the gallery, and peer down at us unseen as we crossed the hall below, came into my mind.

My own voice sounded too loud in the gloom, but I had to ask it.

'Sister, is there any possibility of this place being haunted?'

I felt foolish when I had asked the question. Perhaps she would rebuke me for superstition, or mark me as a cowardly, fanciful type of female.

'There are hauntings of many kinds,' she said, 'and not all of them are to be feared.'

'But here? This place?'

'Sister Hyacinth is at rest,' she said in a tone that was intended to reassure me. 'She was a charming woman, the last soul in the world to be tied to the place of death.'

'Place of death? Here? She died here?'

'I assumed Mother Catherine had told you.' The nun sounded embarrassed now. 'Sister Hyacinth fell from the gallery to the floor here. She was killed instantly, God rest her.'

'She fell down?'

'She must have lost her balance and pitched over the rail,' said Sister Felicity. 'We heard the scream and found her lying here. But she is at rest now.'

I wanted to ask more questions, a hundred more questions, but she was hurrying on, opening a door beyond the one which led to the parlour, and changing the subject gently but firmly.

'You must ask Mother Catherine for details; but come into the guest house now, and let me show you your room.'

4

We were now in the west wing; in a square, panelled apartment with a staircase in the corner. As in the east wing, the rooms led one out of another.

Sister Felicity crossed to the inner door and, opening it, revealed a large, handsomely furnished drawing-room. Beyond this lay an equally imposing parlour and beyond that a dining-room. I tried, and failed, to imagine myself at the head of the long table, eating my meals in solitary state.

'We hoped to build on a little kitchen,' she said regretfully. 'At present all the food is prepared in the big kitchen and carried through on trays, but it's difficult to keep soup hot. There are some excellent books in the drawing-room. If you are fond of reading — '

She gave me a slightly worried look as if she wondered how on earth a young girl would manage to amuse herself. I assured her hastily that I was very fond of reading, and noticed with relief that fires crackled in the grates and that oil lamps glowed in every room.

'We are hoping to have gas installed when we can afford it,' Sister Felicity said. 'If I light these at seven in the evening and come in at ten to extinguish them, would that be convenient? I will leave two of them ready filled for your own personal use so that you may stay up as late as you please.'

I caught another worried glance as if she feared I might take it into my head to stay up all night and hold noisy parties.

'The bedrooms are upstairs.'

She led the way back into the ante-room and ascended the twisting staircase.

We came out into a narrow corridor with four doors opening off it.

'I put you in the largest room. The bed is aired, and I've kindled a fire and lit the lamp. The windows all face inwards over the courtyard.'

She opened the first door and ushered me into a warm and cheerful bedroom. My trunk and satchel had been carried up here, and velvet curtains closed out the night.

'These were the family quarters. I believe the servants slept in the east wing, but we have hung curtains so that we each have a private cell. Mother Catherine's room is above the parlour, but there is no connecting door. The guest house is quite separate as you see.'

I had seen, and felt a tiny prickle of apprehension. To all intents and purposes I would be sleeping alone in a house. I reminded myself that only a wall divided the upper storey of the west wing from Mother Catherine's apartment, and that only the main hall separated us both from the east wing where the nuns were housed. But a wall is solid, and the hall was large, dim, and echoing.

'Mother Catherine would be pleased if you would take a cup of coffee with her in the parlour,' Sister Felicity said.

'Shall I come down now? I can unpack later.'

And look into the other bedrooms and under the beds and behind the hangings, my mind mocked.

We came down the stairs again into the main hall where Sister Felicity tapped on the parlour door, opened it at the sound of a raised voice, and stood aside to let me pass.

'Miss Dean, please come in and make yourself at home.' The Prioress drew me within and bowed a dismissal to Sister Felicity. 'Have you inspected the guest house? Do you think you can be comfortable there for a little while?'

'Yes, indeed.' My voice must have sounded over-hearty for she gave me a shrewd glance

55

as she indicated a chair drawn up to the now blazing fire. However she made no comment but busied herself in pouring coffee.

'Help yourself to milk and sugar,' she invited. 'And please eat all the little cakes. Sister Elizabeth swears the recipe for them was handed down in her family for generations.'

'Sister Elizabeth does the cooking?'

'Yes, and most of the marketing. Sister Felicity is in charge of the linen and looks after the guest house. She is also the infirmarian. Sister Joan is her assistant. Sister Perpetua manages the rest of the cleaning; but the novices help her when they are not receiving formal instruction from Mother Marie.'

'And the others?'

I was prying into matters that were not my concern, I knew.

'Sister Damian is our gardener. Sister Marguerite, and Sister Bridget teach at the little school in Hepton.'

'They leave the convent!'

'We are not an enclosed Order,' the Prioress said, looking amused. 'We each have to perform some task which will help to support the Community in addition to our regular duties within the Convent. Sister Marguerite and Sister Bridget are excused

Convent duties as they have full-time teaching posts, and Mother Marie and I deal with internal matters, and so cannot undertake outside work, but the others all contribute financially. Sister Elizabeth bakes birthday cakes and wedding cakes for example, and Sister Perpetua writes little verses for the local newspaper.'

'You all sound very busy,' I said lamely.

'Sister Hyacinth had arranged to work part-time in the hospital at Hepton with Sister Joan,' Mother Catherine said. 'Unfortunately she had not begun her duties when she died. I believe she would have made herself very useful, but it is not for us to question God's Will.'

It occurred to me that the Prioress had been talking a great deal without telling me anything very important. The thought gave me the courage to probe further.

'Can you tell me about Sister Hyacinth? About her death? She was, after all, a friend.'

'She fell,' Mother Catherine said, slowly, reluctantly. 'It was an accident, a terrible, tragic accident that nobody could have foreseen. She lost her balance and fell over the rail of the gallery, the one at the back of the hall. We can only be thankful that she couldn't have suffered.'

'Is the gallery unsafe?'

'On the contrary, it's structurally quite sound. Of course it has been strengthened in the past, and reinforced again within the last fifty years. But Sister Hyacinth fell over the rail. It is too low for safety, and for that reason I forbade the Sisters to go up there.'

'Then what was Sister Hyacinth doing there then?' I demanded.

The nun's pale, aristocratic features tightened.

'I cannot tell you, Miss Dean,' she said, after an instant's pause. 'Sister Hyacinth certainly was aware of the rule even though she had been here for such a short time. There was nothing in the world to have taken her up to that gallery, or nothing I can imagine that would excuse such disobedience.'

But it was more than the thought of Sister Hyacinth's disobedience that troubled the Prioress.

'Helen — I mean before she became Sister Hyacinth — was a very sensible, cheerful person. She would never have — '

'She was a charming woman with an excellent record,' Mother Catherine said. 'It was an accident. Why she went up to the gallery in the first place, we'll never know, but I'm convinced she was not deliberately disobedient. It was a lapse, a momentary inattention, that's all. And it ended tragically.'

'She was alone when it happened?'

'We were at evening recreation. There was a sudden, terrible scream. We ran out and she was — lying there.'

She opened her thin hands as if Helen had just dropped between them.

'Is it certain she fell from the gallery?' I asked. 'If she was alone — '

'The doctor confirmed that her injuries had been caused by the impact after falling from a great height. I went up to the gallery the following morning when it was light. There were some threads from her habit caught on a jagged bit of wood on the rail.'

'Surely there was an inquest?'

'Three days afterwards. A simple verdict of accident. We didn't mention the fact that she had disobeyed a rule. The question never came up.'

'But didn't they want to know why she went up there?'

'Oh, yes, indeed. Sister Joan made the suggestion that she might have heard a noise, or gone up to fasten a window. Those windows can all be swung open, though one or two are a trifle rusty. The Coroner accepted the suggestion as a probability.'

'It seems so impossible, that she should have died,' I said, feeling suddenly miserable.

'Everything possible was done,' Mother Catherine said. 'We had the customary services, the customary seven days mourning. Tomorrow you'll wish to pay your respects at her graveside, I'm sure.' Her tone changed and lightened. 'But we must try to make your stay here a pleasant one, Miss Dean. You do feel you would be comfortable in the guest house?'

'I don't think I shall enjoy eating all my meals alone,' I admitted, revealing a small worry so that the greater one might remain hidden. 'Wouldn't it be possible for some other arrangement to be made?'

'That thought had already occurred to me.' Mother Catherine sounded relieved to be able to change the subject. 'I was wondering if you would object to taking some of your meals in the refectory with us. You would have received the same food as we eat ourselves, anyway.'

I nodded, holding back the wry thought that eating in silent company might be almost as dreary as eating alone.

'You would probably enjoy breakfast in your own room but we would welcome your company at dinner time and for supper. We eat at one o'clock, and at six in the evening. If you are making any other arrangements at any time, perhaps you would let Sister Elizabeth know?'

Mother Catherine still looked strained despite her obvious attempt to be cheerful. I wondered if the death of one of her nuns would have engraved such dark shadows under her eyes. Or did the responsibilities of her position cause the tension in that slim frame and thin hands?

'You have a regular routine, I suppose?'

I had uncomfortable visions of inadvertently interrupting a prayer meeting or something of the kind.

'A very simple one. We are so isolated here that it's quite impossible to have a daily Mass, but Father Justin comes over from Hepton on Sundays to hear our confessions and offer Mass. On other mornings we rise at six, tidy our cells and then go into chapel to read our Office and to offer up an hour's mental prayer before breakfast.'

There was a gleam of humour in her eyes as she saw my barely concealed dismay.

'After breakfast we go to our various tasks, speaking only when it's absolutely necessary. That rule is waived when there are visitors present, so do please feel free to talk to the Sisters whenever you meet them. Dinner is at one, as I said. Between two and three we read or sew or write letters if we are in the house. Then we return to our duties until prayers at five-thirty. Supper is at six and then we have recreation until eight o'clock. After that we have prayers for an hour in chapel and then, unless we have other duties, we retire.'

It sounded so quiet and serene. Yet, just over a week ago, the gentle routine had been violently shattered by the death of one of the nuns, by the death of the young woman who had been kind to a child she saw for only two months out of every summer. And somewhere in the house was another young woman who gazed, anguished, wringing her hands, from an upper window.

'This is quite a small community, isn't it?' I said, sipping the last of my quite excellent coffee.

'Only twelve. It's a tradition in the Order that, as far as possible, each of our houses should contain twelve Sisters, just as Our Lord had twelve disciples. Of course it's not always possible to keep the numbers exactly correct. We are only eleven now.'

I was ticking them off in my mind when I realized Mother Catherine had risen and was holding out her hand. A key dangled from her fingers.

'This is the key to the guest house. You will be able to lock yourself in. Sister Felicity has the other key so she will be able to bring over your breakfast without disturbing you. If you need anything at any time there is a bell in your room. I'm assured that one tug on the rope will be heard in any corner of the house.'

'Thank you. I shall look forward to seeing you tomorrow, Mother Catherine.'

She opened the door and I passed through it into the dark hall. It seemed even larger when I stood there alone. The gallery was barely discernible and the walls stretched up into infinity.

I stood for a few minutes looking up towards the pale rectangles of gleaming glass, a row of eyes looking down upon the stone floor and the big oaken door. Helen had climbed up to the gallery in the dimness of evening. She had disobeyed an explicit rule and gone up into the gallery; and fallen from the rail down to the flagstones.

I considered the possibility that she might have jumped. Even a young woman who had entered the religious life might conceivably go out of her mind and put an end to her existence, I supposed. But my instincts rejected it. Helen had always been so cheerful, so sure of herself. That was why I had enjoyed being with her. She had represented the easy, undemanding security I had never known with my father. Even though we had not met for six years I couldn't imagine that she had changed so completely.

Then it *must* have been an accident. A trailing habit, a too low rail, a sudden attack of vertigo. It must have been an accident. I tried to imagine Sister Hyacinth, attracted by some noise below, leaning out and losing her balance and pitching forward. I could only imagine Helen Mayhew as I had seen her during that last summer we had met, leaning far out over London Bridge with the wind blowing her curly hair.

'Do be careful, Helen! You might fall in!'

'Not I! When I was your age I used to climb trees and balance on the top branches. I'd do it now, only I might be arrested for showing my petticoats.'

It had *not* been an accident! I had no proof, only a remembered conversation and a deep, inward certainty.

I went through the door which separated the west wing from the main hall. Sister Felicity had already extinguished the lamps in the downstairs rooms, but there was one burning on a small table at the foot of the stairs. I took it up, and having locked the door, went up to the narrow corridor with the four bedrooms opening off it.

The three farther rooms were well-furnished bedrooms, carpeted and curtained, and unoccupied. I was foolish enough to make quite certain of that fact by peering behind the curtains and opening the empty cupboards.

Back in the room that had been assigned to me, I unpacked my trunk and changed into nightgown and wrap. There were two windows in my room with the large, velvet-hung bed between them. I drew aside the curtain at the right-hand window and looked out through tiny panes of glass into the darkness.

The window faced inwards over a garden. I could see it dimly when I held up the lamp, and could also see, by craning my neck a trifle, the long dark mass of the main façade jutting at right angles. I could see too answering reflections cast by my lamp and falling on the stained-glass windows.

At the other side of the garden, opposite me, the shuttered windows of the east wing blocked my view. There was no sound but the faint rustling of small night creatures as they crept busily through the grass.

The fire still burned faintly. I went over and warmed my hands at it, trying not to listen to the silence. There was a carafe of lemonade and a tin of biscuits on a small table. I drank some of the lemonade but the snapping of my own teeth on a biscuit made me jump.

When I got into bed and lay down my room seemed larger, dwarfing me as I gazed round from the shelter of fleecy blankets and eiderdown pillows.

It took me a moment to summon up the resolution to put out the light, and when I was plunged into darkness the limits of the room receded beyond my vision and I pulled up the blankets to create a haven of safety in an immensity of gloom.

I slept at last and dreamed, as usual, of Pierre. I could exclude him from my waking thoughts but in dreams he returned, smiling at me and always, always out of reach I knew myself to be asleep and struggled to awake, to free myself from the smiling dream, but my body remained inert, held down like lead to the pillow I could feel at the edge of my mind.

There was a whispering in the room, beyond the figure of Pierre who wavered and shrank to the size of a doll.

'Who are you? Who are you? Tell me your name!'

I answered, or thought I answered, 'Verona Dean. Who are you?'

'Lady Eadgyth. I am Lady Eadgyth.'

And then came a trill of delighted laughter that jerked me completely into a terrified and trembling wakefulness.

I was cold with the sweat that drenched me from head to foot. My teeth and fists were clenched so tightly that it was an effort to unloose them. I lay, staring into the limitless dark, trying to accustom my eyes to the shapes in the room. The fire had gone out completely and there was a chill in the apartment.

I pushed aside the bedclothes and swung my legs over the side of the bed. I had left the lamp and the big box of lucifers on the table at the side.

My hand ventured out, gripping the sharp edge of the table, brushing over the polished surface, grasping the box. The lucifers made a little, rattling sound within as I lifted it and slid back the lid.

Somewhere in the big, dark room, someone *or something* giggled on a high, excited note. My hand jerked so violently that the box flew out of it and lucifers cascaded over the floor. Then I was kneeling on the thick carpet, my fingers scrabbling for the elusive pieces of wood, my breath sobbing.

I had found one, and found also the box, but I could not tell how many minutes had passed.

I dragged myself up and struck a little, shaking light that danced up and down as I applied it to the wick of the dim outline that was the lamp. It flickered for an instant and then streamed up. My hands cupped the glass globe and lifted it to the base.

The darkness fled and the room dwindled into brightness. I sat down again, reaching for slippers and wrap. My eyes moved, slowly and fearfully, round the room.

I was the only person there, but in sudden feverish activity I began to search, swishing back the curtains, burrowing into the recesses of the large wardrobe, even lying flat in order to examine the space under the bed.

There was nothing. The windows were closed tightly and the door was shut. But it could have been opened silently as I lay sleeping.

I went over to it and stared at the polished panels of wood. The idea that someone waited for me on the other side made me tremble again.

I grasped the handle firmly and twisted it, but the door stayed firm, resisting my pull. For a moment I felt relief mingle with my exasperation. To have been locked in betokened a living, human agent. It was something with which I felt competent to deal.

Then my eyes fell on the little bolt drawn across into its socket. The door had been locked not from the outside with a key, but from within by means of the little bolt.

I slid it back, opened the door, lifted the lamp, went out into the narrow corridor. Slowly, carefully, dreading the recurrence of that high giggle, I searched the three empty bedrooms again.

I descended the stairs and went through the lower rooms. They were empty and the main door was still locked, the key reposing still in my pocket.

When I returned to the bedroom, I drew the curtains and left the lamp burning, but it was grey dawn before I closed my eyes and my sleep was full of whispers.

5

I awoke to bright sunlight and a tapping on my door. At my sleepy 'Come in,' Sister Felicity entered, carrying a laden tray. She put it down on the table, refrained from staring at the still-flickering lamp, and directed a broad smile towards me.

'I hope you won't mind my disturbing you, Miss Dean?' she said. 'You've certainly slept well. Most people do when they come here. It must be the air.'

'What time is it?'

'Past ten o'clock. I brought a tray up at eight and knocked then, but you must have been fast asleep. Will you excuse me now? I'll come up later for the tray.'

'Sister!' I struggled upright in the big bed. 'Sister, who is Lady Eadgyth?'

'I believe she was the mistress of the house,' the nun said placidly.

'Was?'

'About four hundred years ago, I think. That was when the main part of the house was built. Eat your breakfast before it goes cold, Miss Dean.'

She gave me another pleasant smile and went out.

Only the guilty thought that she had wasted one tray already forced me to eat the bacon and eggs, the toast and apricot preserve. To my surprise I discovered myself to be ravenously hungry. Fright must have an effect upon the digestion, I thought wryly, as I drank the rest of the excellent coffee.

In the bright sunshine, the events of the previous night seemed completely fantastic. Sooner or later I would have to examine what had happened, to lay it out piece by piece in my mind.

I stacked the used dishes on the tray and began to dress, choosing a checked wool of pink and grey. It crossed my mind that I ought perhaps to wear mourning for Helen, but she had been no relative and, in any event, my grief at her death had been pushed into the background by my curiosity at the manner of it.

It occurred to me that I might do worse than discover the history of the Lady Eadgyth who had been mistress here four hundred years before. At that time, only the main part of the house had been standing and yet my visitor of the previous night had been in the west wing. I was not certain but I doubted if ghosts ever explored newer parts of a building or had the ability to draw bolts.

When I came down into the main hall one of the novices, the bespectacled girl called Sister Paul, was washing the floor with a great deal of energy. I paused and enquired if it would be possible to go into the garden.

'Oh, yes, indeed. This is the quickest way.' She indicated a low door beneath the gallery, and returned energetically to her work.

I stepped over to it and lifted the latch. A second later I was in the garden I had seen from my window the previous night. The space was bounded to left and right by the west and east wings and closed in on the fourth side by a high yew-hedge. There were a few flower-beds and a semi-circle of lawn, but most of the ground appeared to be given over to the cultivation of vegetables. It was neat and characterless, with little to attract the eye.

I wandered aimlessly down the path towards the hedge. There was no sign of Sister Damian who was, I had been told, the gardener. Everything looked placid and peaceful in the sunlight. Somebody shook a mop vigorously out of an upper window in the east wing. It was a gesture of reassuring normality.

Heartened by it, without quite knowing why, I pushed open a barred gate set in the thick hedge and stepped out on to the curving moor. The breeze was sharper here, probably because the high yew acted as a windbreak in the garden.

The ground rose and fell in a series of green waves, watered by narrow streams that meandered lazily down the slopes and gathered themselves into tiny pools.

I ascended to the crest of the nearest ridge and looked round with delight at the gleams of gold and the duskiness of purple, mingling with the emerald where gorse and heather overlaid the grass. Below me, where the mauve shaded into brown, a square white house nestled against a sharp cliff that rose abruptly against the skyline.

I longed for palette, brushes, easels and canvas, for all the mundane useful objects out of which the artist creates, or just fails to create, the half-remembered vision in the mind. After lunch — dinner as they called it here — I would come out and make a preliminary sketch.

I swung round, feeling eyes upon me, and saw the young man who had carried my trunk the previous day. This morning he shouldered a pitchfork but evidently had no intention of using it, for he leaned at ease against the gate, staring at me with the sort of open admiration more usually displayed by Continental men.

Annoyed and aware of the colour rising in my face, I said sharply, 'Have you no work to do?'

'Aye,' he returned indifferently.

'Then might it not be a good idea to begin it?' I suggested.

'Aye, if tha wishes it.'

He gave me his attractive, lop-sided grin and lounged off, whistling. I felt my annoyance die away as I watched him. It was foolish of me to make an enemy, when a little friendliness on my part might have ensured some information.

I stepped after him, raising my voice a trifle.

'That house down there? To whom does it belong?'

'That house?'

'I fail to see any other,' I said acidly. 'Who lives there?'

'That's Shaw's Cottage,' he said over his shoulder. 'Shaws live there.'

'Who or what are Shaws?'

'Folk, same as t'other folk. They used t'live in *Minstrel's Leap* till the nuns came.'

I would have liked to question him further, but I was afraid to encourage his obvious familiarity. He gave me another long, considering look and slouched away again.

I turned in the opposite direction and

strolled on, letting the breeze ruffle my hair and enjoying the feel of the soft spikes of green against my ankles. I wished I could take off my shoes but there was the possibility that the young man might return.

I had gone some distance when I saw another figure climbing towards me. It was a woman, clad in a figured pelisse and dress of dark blue and white, with a slightly unfashionable bonnet of chip straw on her white hair.

'Miss Dean?' As she came up to me she held out a gloved hand and smiled.

'It seems everybody knows my name,' I commented as we shook hands.

'News travels swiftly in this part of the world,' she said. 'I am Laura Cartwright. I live down at Shaw Cottage.'

'But I thought the Shaws — ?'

'Mr. Shaw was my cousin. After my husband's death I made my home with the family,' she explained. 'I'm on my way to the convent with some groceries. I like to contribute a little something now and then to the Sisters. Were you comfortable in the guest house?'

'Very comfortable,' I said politely.

'The Sisters are most hospitable, are they not?' she commented. 'Such a hard life for a girl to choose, I always think. And it's such a steep climb.'

She let her glance stray wistfully to the covered basket on her arm.

'I can save you the rest of the climb by delivering your groceries myself,' I offered.

'Oh, my dear, I couldn't possibly — oh, how very kind of you!'

She relinquished her burden with no more than token resistance and gave me an embarrassed little smile.

'There seems to be so much to do and it's quite impossible to find decent girls to live-in these days. I was not brought up to baking and sewing, you understand.'

'No, indeed.'

She had the look, I thought, of a faded gentlewoman. Her tall, thin figure was rigidly corseted and there were lines around her mouth and eyes that hinted at past sorrows.

'*Minstrel's Leap*? It's a very lovely house,' I said.

'Very old and very lovely,' she agreed.

'I wondered why it was called by that name. It's unusual, isn't it? I mean, there must be a story.'

I looked at her hopefully, and after an instant's hesitation she folded her gloved hands together and gave a series of nods.

'Oh yes, a most romantic tale. Of course, it is not, I fear, a very edifying one. Morals were very lax in the early sixteenth century. I blame Lady Eadgyth. Of all people she should have known better, for she came from a very well-connected family. One can only assume that her parents had neglected her when she was at an impressionable age.'

'But what exactly did she do?'

'She fell in love with a minstrel,' said Laura Cartwright in a shocked tone. 'It was very wrong of her because she was already married to the owner of the house. It was not called *Minstrel's Leap* then, of course, but Shaw Grange. The Shaw of the time was a certain Sir William Shaw. He was knighted on the accession of King Henry VIII and built the house — the main part of it — shortly afterwards. That was when he married Eadgyth. There was a considerable difference in their ages, though that does not excuse her behaviour.'

'With the minstrel?'

She nodded her white head.

'He used to ride over, and visit the Lady Eadgyth.' She pursed her mouth up coyly. 'Sir William was often away from home, dispensing justice, for these parts were very lawless in those days. Unhappily, he came home early one day, before the servants had time to warn their mistress. She was up in the gallery with her — with the minstrel.'

'What happened?' I clasped my own hands tightly together.

'The young man jumped through one of the windows that open off the gallery. Not the present windows — they date from the seventeenth century. At that time there were trees growing at the back of the house. He leapt into the branches of one of them and then down to his horse, and was away before they could catch him.'

'And Lady Eadgyth? What happened to her?'

'As far as I know she forgot her wild days and settled down to be a good and faithful wife,' Laura Cartwright said disappointingly. 'But the house was known as *Minstrel's Leap* from that day on.'

I had expected more than this tame anti-climax.

'Didn't Sir William *mind* about his wife's lover?' I asked.

'He was very fond of his wife,' Laura Cartwright reproved. 'He may have reproached her from time to time afterwards.'

'Or stayed home oftener,' I said.

Laura Cartwright gave me another faintly shocked glance.

'I was wondering, Miss Dean, if you wouldn't consider it presumptuous of me on such short acquaintance, whether you would have supper with me tonight. I assume you will be staying in this district for a while?'

'For a month at least,' I nodded.

'Shall we say seven o'clock then? We usually dress.'

'I shall look forward to it.'

'I'll arrange for Simon to pick you up at six-thirty. The track over the moors is often difficult to follow after the day-light has faded.'

She gave my arm two or three little pats and went briskly away again, moving straight back over the green and gold and purple moor.

I turned back towards the high yew hedge, the basket heavy on my arm. There was no sign of the insolent young man, and I was annoyed with myself for the momentary disappointment that cast down my spirits.

As I walked back through the garden, a door in the east wing opened and Sister Elizabeth came out.

'I saw you through the kitchen window, Miss Dean. Would you like a cup of tea before dinner?' she enquired.

I shook my head and handed over the basket.

'I met Mrs. Cartwright on her way here,' I said.

'And she has sent groceries! Always so kind!'

'She has invited me down to Shaw Cottage for supper tonight,' I said. 'Will that be inconvenient?'

'Not in the least,' she assured me. 'You will probably get an excellent meal. Mrs. Cartwright is a superb cook.'

She gave me a little wave of the hand and whisked back into the kitchen.

I went more soberly to the little door in the centre of the main block and passed beneath the gallery into the great, stone-flagged hall.

Here I stood for a long time looking up at the gallery. Sunlight poured through the stained-glass windows and columns of dust danced high above me in the shafts of sunlight.

Yet the gallery still had a dim and insubstantial aspect. I tried to recall everything that had been told to me by Mrs. Cartwright, to fill the hall with the people who had played their parts in that long-ago drama.

They would have been in the gallery, these lovers. The minstrel would have drawn Eadgyth far back into the shadowy corner between the wall and the end window. In the hall where I now stood servants would have been passing to and fro. Perhaps a fire had been burning. And then the great oaken door would have been flung open, and Sir William Shaw had marched in, his spurs jangling, his eyes darting suspiciously from side to side.

The minstrel — I thought of him as young and handsome — had turned in a flash, leaping through the open casement into the high branches of a tree, and then down into the saddle of his waiting horse. But for Eadgyth there had been no such escape.

Had she stood, watching her lover as he clung to the branches, praying that he might get away? Or had she come forward to the rail of the gallery, leaning forward with her hair hanging loose and calling smiling words of welcome to her husband?

Perhaps it had been that way, for Sir William had forgiven her and she had become a true and faithful wife. I wondered what had happened to the lover. Had he too settled down and grown old and respectable? But in Eadgyth's mind surely he had stayed reckless and handsome, never ageing, never more attainable.

A bell clanged, the signal for dinner, as I realized when I looked at my fob watch. I had spent much longer than I realized both out on the moor and in the hall.

I went through into the stone-walled refectory. It seemed less strange today to take my place on the bench next to the black-robed figures. Sister Bridget and Sister Marguerite were absent. I presumed they had their midday meal over in the school where they taught.

Our own meal was as silent as before, enlivened only by Sister Joan's sharp voice reading a portion from the life of some saint or other. The saint had come to an unusually blood-thirsty end. The nuns listened placidly, chewing their beef puddings and sipping water.

After dinner I went up to my room to collect the materials I would need for my sketch. If it turned out well I would give it to the Sisters as a parting present.

My bed had been made, the grate cleaned and the fire re-laid. The guest house was warm and sunny.

I tied a scarf over my hat and took up my pencils and the larger of my two sketching blocks. Then I went out into the garden.

The place was silent again and the silence irritated me. There were questions to be asked, explanations to be demanded, but I could not penetrate the gentle, well-bred silence.

In the old days, whenever I had been anxious or worried, my father had always urged me to paint a picture.

'Don't keep trouble locked up in your head, girl. Let it flow out through the tips of your fingers. Release it into your work!'

He had practised what he preached. His own work had become progressively angrier and more violent, and the more he let trouble flow through his fingertips, the more obsessed he became with his own problems until, by the end, one could not have told whether the paintings reflected him or he reflected the paintings.

What was certain was that few people had admired his work and fewer had bought it. And in the very end, at the last when we stayed three months in Paris, he had deliberately courted failure. Perhaps he had known what it would be like, that grand climax. But he could not have foreseen my own stumbling through those boulevards on fire with chestnut trees to the tall, narrow house with the shell fanlight.

I had passed through the gate, had seated myself on the ridge, and was drawing the outlines of the surrounding landscape. And at the same time I was running through those streets, my heart hammering, my lips shaping the name of Pierre.

I put down my pencil and reached into the satchel. My father had enjoyed one particular vice and taught me to enjoy it too. I still had a supply of the thin brown, Spanish cigarillos we had smoked together after the blazing heat of the Mediterranean day dwindled into a brief blue twilight.

I shielded the flame of the lucifer with my hand and drew in the fragrant smoke. I had never dared to indulge in the habit in public, but there were times when my nerves craved relief.

The drawing on the pad was a faint symphony of wavering lines, culminating in the tiny house. Near to the house was the outline of a female figure, looking down towards the cottage.

The grass behind me rustled and I turned my head and saw the young gardener. My first annoyed thought was that he had caught me smoking, my next the equally annoyed realization that the spectacle evidently amused him. Because of that my manner was more flustered than I had intended.

'Haven't you any work to do? I came out here to be alone!'

'I reckoned that!' he returned insolently, his eyes on the thin column of smoke that rose up from between my fingers.

'Before you go,' I stressed the words slightly, 'I believe you're to drive me down to Shaw Cottage this evening. Did Mrs. Cartwright tell you?'

'Aye, she said summat o'th sort.'

'At six-thirty promptly.'

'In't buggy,' he agreed, and instead of going away came closer and bent over to examine my drawing. He came so close that the straw he held between his teeth brushed the side of my neck.

I moved away slightly as crimson warmed my cheeks.

'Are you interested in art?'

'Yon lass'll never fit in't front door of that house!' he said, shifting the straw to the other side of his mouth.

'She doesn't belong,' I said shortly.

I had only just discovered the fact myself. The figure was me, I supposed, looking into a warmth and a security that could never be. The discovery depressed me so much that tears came into my eyes.

'Why do you hang about here? What do you want?' I said harshly.

'Thought I'd make sure tha doesna start a fire,' he said.

'Very considerate of you, but I'm not in the habit of setting light to myself!' I retorted.

'Mebbe not, but tha might put flame to t'moor. That's sweet grass.'

Such a comment was quite unforgivable. I scrambled to my feet, pushing my things back into the satchel, grinding out the half-finished cigarette under my heel. Then I whirled about, clutching my skirt in one hand. My face was burning so fiercely that I dare not turn round, but I heard him chuckling quite audibly as I stumbled away.

6

For the rest of the afternoon I was left in peace. The obnoxious Simon had apparently taken himself off and I sketched at my ease from a different vantage point until the sun sank and I became aware that I was cramped and chilled.

I made my way back to the guest house through the silence that seemed to enfold me when I entered *Minstrel's Leap*. Such quietness would have pleased me under normal circumstances, but it served now only as a space in which small fears could grow into greater terrors.

I tried to push my memory of the giggling voice and the girl at the upper window, and Helen's accident that could have been no accident, to the back of my mind, and to concentrate instead upon dressing for the evening. Laura Cartwright had made a point of telling me that dress would be formal.

I had only one gown that would fit into such a category. It was of rose pink silk, round-necked with tiny sleeves and a ruched skirt over a half-hoop. I had bought the dress for — but that wasn't important any longer. I might as well wear it to grace an evening with a middle-aged lady.

I combed and coiled my hair and added the spray of pink roses my father had bought for me. I had destroyed Pierre's gifts long before, the previous summer, but I had been wearing the dress and the spray of flowers on that evening. I made a face at myself in the mirror that had thoughtfully been provided for me in the bedroom, and reached for my cloak.

As I came down the narrow stairs, I met Sister Felicity emerging from the suite of rooms on the ground floor. She gave me an admiring look.

'That's a beautiful dress, Miss Dean!' she exclaimed. 'I've always loved pink, especially on dark-haired people. Sister Elizabeth tells me that you'll be out this evening.'

'At Mrs. Cartwright's.'

'I'll build up the fire in your bedroom, and leave the lamp. Have you got your key?'

I patted the small velvet bag I carried.

'I'll wish you a pleasant evening then.'

She bustled back into the other room with less than the usual gliding grace. It struck me that she was playing at being housewife rather like a little girl who plays at being mother with her dolls.

As I passed into the hall the main door

opened and Simon poked in a tousled head, apparently in search of me.

'Buggy's out front, miss,' he said.

'I'm quite ready.'

I swept past him with my nose in the air but was obliged to accept his aid up to my seat. He whistled his way to the driving side and swung himself up, clicking his tongue to the horse.

We made the journey in silence, for I had not the faintest desire to engage in conversation, and my companion occupied his time in crooning to the horse and in whistling loudly in a manner calculated to irritate the most placid person.

The path was a wide and wandering track etched out across the swells and billows of the moor. Here and there I was forced to hold on tightly to the edge of my seat, and once a sudden lurch sent me almost toppling across the driver's lap. I jerked upright but he met my glare with a flash of white teeth and a cocked eyebrow that made me long to slap him.

Within a quarter of an hour we had reached the house I had seen from the back of *Minstrel's Leap*. It was larger than I had imagined it to be, a square white building set against the ridged cliff and surrounded by a pleasant garden. The colours had faded from the world and I could catch the fragrance of night-scented stock.

The buggy stopped at a neat white gate and Simon leaned across, apparently with the intention of assisting me down, but I ignored his outstretched arm and scrambled down myself.

'Thank you,' I said, briefly. 'I shall expect you to be ready to take me back.'

He made no reply but flapped the reins across the back of the horse and grinned over his shoulder as it ambled away. I pushed open the gate and went briskly up the flagged path. Before I reached the front door it opened and a welcoming shaft of light beamed out.

'Do come in, Miss Dean,' Laura Cartwright invited. 'I heard the buggy clip-clopping across the path. Such a friendly sound, I always think!'

Although she had opened the door herself, she had obviously dressed for company in a trailing gown of grey lace with a bustle, though in London bustles were quite out of fashion that year. Her white hair was piled up high and augmented by a false fringe on which a brooch glittered.

I stepped into a narrow hall where she relieved me of my cloak and led the way, still chattering, into a square, panelled room where a fire blazed.

'Do sit down, Miss Dean. It gets so chilly in the evenings. Have you spent a pleasant day? It's very quiet here for a young lady. Now you must meet my charge. Edith, my dear, will you come and shake hands?'

A slight figure had risen from a high-backed chair and advanced towards me with outstretched hand. I held out my hand automatically while my senses reeled. This girl in a demure muslin gown with her hair curled into tight ringlets was the girl I had seen at the upper window on the previous day.

I opened my mouth but the slim fingers gripped mine warningly as the girl spoke in a light, breathless voice.

'I am Edith Shaw, Miss Dean. Cousin Laura told me that you would be coming this evening. I'm delighted to meet you. We have so few visitors here.'

'I'm staying at the guest house,' I said, more to cover a pause than anything for she was surely aware of that already.

'We used to live at *Minstrel's Leap*,' Edith said. 'I never go there now. Never!'

'We feel the nuns appreciate their privacy,' Laura Cartwright said. 'What a pretty dress, Miss Dean. I think pink looks so charming with dark hair.'

'Sister Felicity said the same thing.'

I accepted a seat by the fire.

'Felicity, Felicity,

'Oh, such duplicity!'

For a moment I thought I had imagined the couplet, but Edith chanted it again in a high, sing-song voice.

'Do be quiet,' Laura Cartwright said, a trifle acidly. 'It's not polite to make fun of the poor Sisters.'

'I've seen that rhyme before, or heard it,' Edith protested.

'Or imagined it,' said a voice from the doorway. 'You mustn't take any notice of my little sister, Miss Dean. She is full of fads and fancies.'

It was fortunate that I was sitting down already because at this second shock my legs would assuredly have buckled underneath me. The gentleman who had entered was tall and impeccably dressed in high stock and well-cut evening suit. I had seen him last grinning at me from the driving seat of the buggy. Now he bowed ceremoniously, speaking in an accent that held only the faintest trace of Northern flatness.

'It's pleasant to be able to welcome you to Shaw Cottage. I see that Cousin Laura has made you comfortable, but you must allow me to offer you a glass of sherry. If we lived in a more emancipated age, I might be tempted to offer you a small cigar to accompany it, but as it is, I shall venture to enjoy a cigar myself later. You won't complain if the smoke drifts your way?'

I could only glare at him helplessly.

'Simon, dear,' Laura Cartwright exclaimed, 'what nonsense you do talk! He talks the most shocking nonsense, Miss Dean. You must not believe the half of what he says!'

'I won't,' I said grimly.

'If you'll excuse me for a moment I must go and see about the meal,' Laura Cartwright said. 'Edith, why don't you play one of your charming pieces on the pianoforte?'

'I'll play when I've eaten, not before!' said Edith in such a sulky tone that I gaped at her.

'Music always sounds sweeter after supper,' her brother said, apparently unaware of, or indifferent to, her rudeness.

'I heard some very fine playing last night. Sister Bridget entertained us at recreation,' I said.

'Ah, the little Irish one with the blue eyes. She and Sister Marguerite teach over in Hepton,' he said.

'Simon takes them to the school every day and brings them back again in the afternoon,' Edith said. 'And he does all kinds of odd jobs for them.'

'A paragon, evidently,' I said.

'I hardly like to boast,' Simon murmured.

'You must force yourself, Mr. Shaw,' I returned sweetly.

'Oh, you mustn't be so stuffy!' Edith cried. 'Call him Simon. Everybody calls him Simon hereabouts, even Mother Catherine. And we will call you — what is your first name?'

'Verona.'

'That's a pretty name!' she exclaimed.

'Extremely pretty.' He gave me a long, sweeping glance.

'The meal is ready.'

Laura Cartwright, a trifle flushed, due, I guessed, to last-minute exertions in the kitchen, came back into the room.

We went across the narrow hall into a dining-room, heavily draped and cooler than the room where we had been sitting. An oval table had been laid for four people and a casserole steamed in the centre of the white cloth.

'Just a simple ragout,' Laura Cartwright fluted.

'That's French for stew,' Simon said kindly.

'Unless it contains fish when it would be known as bouillabaisse,' I said with equal kindness.

'Have you been abroad?' Edith asked.

'I've lived on the Continent for most of my

life, until my father died last year,' I explained.

'Cousin Laura went to Paris once and took a cookery course just before she got married,' Edith said.

'An indispensable preparation for wedlock,' Simon declared.

'Do you cook, Verona?' Edith asked.

'She draws pictures,' her brother interposed.

'My father was an artist.'

'You didn't tell us that, Simon!'

'A highly respected artist, Cousin Laura,' Simon said. 'Quite avant-garde — wasn't that the expression you used, Verona?'

I crumbled bread and muttered something. It was obvious that he was playing some kind of game with Cousin Laura, and with me. His voice trembled on the edge of laughter. When he looked at Edith, however, his expression softened. She was now cramming food into her mouth as if she had not eaten for days.

'I understand you used to live at *Minstrel's Leap*,' I said.

'We were born and bred there,' Simon said. 'Cousin Laura practically brought us up. Mother died when Edith was seven and Laura came over as housekeeper. She had just lost her own husband, so the arrangement worked very well.'

'My own father and Simon's grandfather were brothers,' Laura said. 'My father died before I was born so we never knew him at all. We spent most of our time with Uncle William.'

'We?'

'My sister and myself. My mother died when I was three. There was an older sister, Jane. There were fourteen years in our age differences so she looked after me until I was ten, and then I came to *Minstrel's Leap* until my own marriage. John and I were not blessed with a family of our own, so I was very pleased to have the chance of taking care of Edith after her own mother died.'

'Father died three years ago,' Edith chipped in. 'It was an — '

'Plum-tart, Verona? I am rather vain of my pastry.'

Laura was scooping clots of cream on to the rosy mounds of pudding.

'*Minstrel's Leap* was a white elephant,' said Simon. 'Last year I decided to cut my losses and hand it over to the Sisters. We came back to Shaw's Cottage.'

'This was my father's house,' Laura said. 'He was the younger brother, you see, but he wanted a home of his own when he married. The actual land is part of the larger estate, so it reverted to Cousin Simon eventually.'

'I want to play the piano! I'm sick of eating,' Edith declared, giving her plate a shove that sent plum juice tipping over the white cloth. 'Cousin Laura, make the coffee!'

I was irritated when, instead of reproving her for her bad manners, Simon said, 'Excellent. We'll come through and listen with pleasure.'

I was most reluctant to hurry my meal, but he was already at the back of my chair, Edith had whisked across the hall, and Laura was piling up plates with a few disconnected words about leaving them for Nancy when she came in the next morning.

In the firelit room, Edith had seated herself at the pianoforte and was thumping out a tune with more energy than talent. Simon drew me over to the window-seat.

'At what hour dost tha need t'buggy?'

'I'll never forgive you,' I said through my teeth. 'I'll never, never forgive you.'

'The fact that you've repeated it leads me to hope we'll be the best of friends by tomorrow,' he said.

'Not with a liar. I could never stand lies,' I said fiercely.

'But I haven't told you any,' he returned with unimpaired good humour. 'It was you who decided I was a — bye the bye, what did you decide I was?'

'A yokel!'

'I thought that was it. My stars, but you looked furious when you got out at the level-crossing! And when you turned round and saw me, I fully expected you to say 'Off with his head!' I was quite relieved when you merely requested me to carry your trunk.'

'You were carrying a scythe!' I said indignantly.

'I do occasionally cut the grass,' he informed me gravely. 'I'm not a wealthy man, my dear, and labour is expensive, so I do a lot of the outdoor work myself and help out at the convent too. I like to keep myself occupied.'

'In pretending to be what you are not.'

'In being what you expected me to be. I was beginning to wonder when anyone would refer to me as Mr. Shaw and give the game away. Ah, coffee! Edith, that was a very pretty piece. You will play again later, won't you?'

'No, I won't, for you never listened,' Edith said, flinging herself into a chair.

'Edith is so temperamental,' said Laura fondly. 'It is really as much as a person can do to keep track of her moods.'

'I have to have moods,' Edith said. 'It's not good for me not to have them. I am now in a very cross mood! Very cross indeed!'

She pouted and pulled one of her long

ringlets across her face.

'Children are often prone to bad humours,' I commented. 'Adults don't usually take any notice of them.'

'I'm not a child. I'm nearly sixteen!'

'Really? I would never have guessed it. Mrs. Cartwright, this is lovely coffee. Do you blend it yourself?'

'Oh, yes indeed. But do please call me Laura. So foolish to stand on ceremony, don't you feel? Do tell us about Paris, my dear. I was there for such a brief time, and so long ago.'

I didn't want to talk about Paris, didn't want to bring back memories of the river winding beneath the arched bridges, the scent of chestnuts along the boulevards. I talked instead about Italy and Spain and the little olive groves of Portugal where we had spent one whole harvest, working with the black-shawled peasants on their strips of land.

'So romantic!' Laura breathed. 'Your father must have been a remarkable person to live among the poor as if he were one of the poor!'

I opened my mouth to explain that there was no pretence about it. We had worked because we had needed the money, but Simon had risen.

'Edith, you must say good night to Verona

now,' he said. 'I have to deliver her back to *Minstrel's Leap.*'

'But you will come again?' Laura also rose, clasping my hands. 'We are starved of polite society here. So many of our old neighbours have moved away from the district, and we don't visit as much as we used to do.'

'There are very few young people about to amuse Edith,' Simon said.

'Edith? It's a family name, I suppose, like Eadgyth?'

'The modern version of it,' Simon agreed. 'We were brought up on that old legend.'

'It's *not* a *legend!*' Edith cried, her lovely face flushing redder than her hair. 'It happened! It happened!'

'Something of the sort probably did,' her brother said.

Edith was not, however, in a mood to be humoured.

'It all happened,' she insisted. 'Lady Eadgyth's heart was broken after the minstrel left. She failed and faded into a shadow.'

'She must have been a rather substantial shadow then,' Simon declared. 'She bore Sir William eight children eventually.'

'Don't listen to him,' Edith entreated. 'You mustn't listen to him. Simon makes fun of everything.'

'I like your version of the story best,' I said,

more to annoy Simon than to please Edith, for I was rapidly coming to the conclusion that she was, at best, a thoroughly spoilt young person.

'There! Verona and I are allies,' she said triumphantly.

Simon had brought my cloak and was draping it about my shoulders. His hands, touching my neck, were warm.

'Good night, Verona. I hope we shall see much more of you,' Laura was repeating. 'We live very simply, I fear, but you won't despise us on that account? Simon, have you brought round the buggy? Oh, do hurry and get it. This is not carriage country, I fear, so we use the buggy for convenience sake.'

Still chattering, she escorted me to the gate and a few minutes later we were retreating into the darkness.

I sat stiffly as far away from my companion as I could get without actually falling out of the buggy. He gave no indication that he had noticed anything amiss however.

'When you come again you must stay longer, but Edith was becoming a trifle over-excited. She is very highly strung and needs to be treated carefully.'

I maintained an eloquent silence.

'Her head is stuffed full of dreams and stories, most of them put there by Cousin

Laura, I'm afraid. She likes to fancy herself as Lady Eadgyth, watching for her lover,' he was continuing.

She likes to frighten people too, I thought sourly. If I have any more visitations the 'ghost' will meet with a warm reception.

'Woulds't tha like it if I talked like t'yokel?' he demanded.

'I would like it if you didn't talk at all,' I said loftily, but my lips were twitching and I heard a giggle escape them.

'I told Cousin Laura that you were an heiress, staying here for the sake of your health,' he informed me.

'You — what!'

'Cousin Laura is so anxious for me to marry money and retrieve the family fortunes,' Simon observed, 'that I think it only right to afford her a little pleasure. Besides, for all I know, you might *be* an heiress.'

'I'm not!' I snapped. 'If it's any of your business, I'm almost penniless.'

'Well, don't let it worry you,' he said kindly. 'A little money would have been useful, but I shall marry you anyway.'

'I would very much enjoy seeing you try,' I gritted. 'As it is I'm tired of your insults and your teasing. So, as we're almost at the convent, you'll oblige me by stopping so that

I can get out. And I can manage perfectly well alone, thank you.'

'I'm sure you can.'

He reined in the horse and waited while I clambered down. His voice followed me as I went up to the main door, mocking, but with a new note in it.

'And I will marry you, Verona Dean. I always carry out my threats.'

7

There were no visitations that night and I slept soundly, waking, rather to my annoyance, with the image of Simon Shaw behind my eyelids. He had, of course, not meant a word of what he had said. Men seldom did mean the flowery compliments they paid to girls. I refused to remember that Simon had not, in fact, paid me any compliments at all.

As I ate my breakfast and dressed, my mind returned, rather guiltily, to Helen. The purpose that had brought me up to *Minstrel's Leap* seemed to have been deflected. My kindly landlady would certainly expect me to find out everything I could. So far I had found out only the manner of Helen's death, but the reason for it eluded me.

I still could not believe it had been an accident, and I didn't think the Prioress believed it either. It would be useless to question her further, however, for she obviously couldn't bear to contemplate even the suggestion that one of her nuns might have committed suicide. Yet she could hardly blame herself. Helen had been at *Minstrel's Leap* for only three weeks and the roots of self-destruction must have been embedded in her nature for a long time before that.

Three weeks. Helen had been at *Minstrel's Leap* for three weeks, after having been transferred from another convent. What was it the Prioress had said? Something about living in communities of twelve like the disciples. I counted the Sisters off in my mind. There was Mother Catherine herself, the Novice Mistress Mother Marie, Sister Elizabeth, Sister Joan, Sister Felicity, Sisters Bridget, Marguerite, Damian, Perpetua, and the two novices, Sister Anne and Sister Paul. Eleven of them since Sister Hyacinth had died. And before Sister Hyacinth had joined them, had they been only eleven then?

I went down to the ground floor and found Sister Felicity on her knees polishing the brass fender. She looked up as I entered and gave me the clear, serene smile that the Sisters seemed to learn during their novitiate.

'Did you have a pleasant evening yesterday?' she enquired.

'I met Edith,' I said.

'Ah, poor child.' The bright smile faded slightly. 'It's very sad for both Mrs. Cartwright and Simon. A heavy responsibility!'

'She comes quite often to the convent?' I said, feeling my way.

'It was her home,' the nun said regretfully. 'She lived here until we moved in, a year ago. It's natural she should spend a great deal of time here. Mrs. Cartwright is somewhat embarrassed by it, I fear, but poor Edith is always welcome here.'

'I was wondering,' I said, drawing in my breath and refusing to allow myself to be sidetracked, 'if you could tell me anything about Sister Hyacinth. She was a friend of mine.'

'A charming person,' the nun said promptly. 'Brisk and lively without being in the least officious or overbearing. We all liked her very much.'

'She — did she replace another Sister?' I ventured.

'Sister Eulalia,' she said, and the smile had completely faded now.

'Was Sister Eulalia transferred?'

'She passed away in January,' Sister Felicity said.

'Passed away? You mean she died?'

'It was very tragic. A great loss. Sister Eulalia was in her early twenties. A great loss.' She spoke flatly, her eyes dull.

'Sister Hyacinth came here to replace Sister Eulalia?'

'We were so pleased when Mother Catherine informed us that we had succeeded

106

in obtaining another Sister and so delighted when she arrived and proved to be so charming,' Sister Felicity said.

'Was Sister Eulalia — a pleasant person?' I asked.

'Very lively. Very up-to-date,' the nun said.

She had turned away and was polishing the grate energetically before I could frame another question.

I was more fortunate in my next encounter. I stepped out into the main hall and met little Sister Bridget hurrying from the east wing.

'Good morning, Sister. Don't you go to school today?' I enquired.

'Not on Wednesdays. The school is for small ones and is open only four days a week. Sure, we'd be murdering the little dears if we didn't get a break from them occasionally,' she twinkled.

'I was going to pay my respects at Sister Hyacinth's grave,' I said.

'Ah, God rest her!' The nun crossed herself. 'Would you like me to come with you, Miss Dean?'

'If you would be so kind, Sister.' I hesitated and then said, 'If it's allowed, may I be called Verona?'

'I'll be delighted,' she said promptly. 'Verona. Would that be short for Veronica now?'

'I was named after the town in Italy,' I explained. 'My father had always wanted to visit the place.'

'And did he get there?'

'We went together before he died. Six months before.'

'Ah, that's satisfying.' She held open the front door and beamed.

'It was too late for him,' I said bitterly. 'He left it too late. He kept putting it off from year to year. We went almost everywhere else but not there. I think he was afraid of being disappointed.'

'And was he?'

'No. It was everything he had expected it to be. But it was too late. He was past healing.'

'And how could you possibly know?' She questioned. 'How can you see deep down into another person's heart when you're wrapped up in your own skin? Sure, we have no right to make judgments.'

'I can judge men,' I said. 'They have soft voices and flint hearts.'

'And aren't you the lucky one to have met all the men in the world!' Sister Bridget gibed. 'If I'd had your advantages, I'd never have left the world!'

We were walking away from the convent, skirting the field through which I had trudged up from the level crossing. The nun pointed ahead to the belt of trees.

'The family burial ground is at the other side of the trees,' she said. 'Simon was very kind. He has allowed us to use the ground for Sister Hyacinth.'

'And for Sister Eulalia?'

'For Sister Eulalia too,' she nodded. 'There is no place really suitable within the house or the enclosed garden. It was very kind, but then we have always received the greatest consideration from the family. People are so kind.'

'Sister Felicity was telling me about Sister Eulalia,' I said mendaciously.

'God rest her!' said Sister Bridget. 'She had only been with us for a year; since she moved here from York.'

'She was very young to die,' I said cautiously.

'Just a simple cold,' Sister Bridget said. 'Of course, Sister Eulalia was always inclined to be a trifle chesty, but Sister Felicity took such good care of her. She used to be a nurse, you know.'

'Sister Felicity? Yes, I know.'

'Poor Sister Eulalia! She was ill for less than a week, which is a mercy in a way, for she didn't suffer very long. But the doctor was surprised. He said he'd never known pneumonia to set in so quickly.'

'Did she neglect the cold?'

'No, indeed. Mother Catherine is very strict on that point. She insists we take care of ourselves sensibly. Sister Eulalia was even moved over to the guest house for fear there might be a danger of infection.' She caught my startled glance, and said, 'Oh, there was nobody staying in the guest house at the time. But that side of the house is so much warmer than the east wing.'

'And Sister Felicity nursed her?'

'And was so upset when the poor Sister died! This is the little burial-plot. The ancestors of the Shaws are buried in the church at Hepton, but for the past hundred years members of the family have been laid to rest here. Isn't it a pretty place now?'

She pointed to the grey tombs clustered beyond the trees in a hollow of the moor. They were obviously old, most of them tilted and moss-encrusted, with here and there the bareness of new stone. A little apart from the rest were two mounds marked by crosses, one grass-brown, the other still earth-brown.

Sister Bridget moved tactfully away and began pulling weeds from one of the older tombs. I stared down at the two graves and the crosses, each marked only with the painted initials of H.M. and E.F.

'Helen or Hyacinth Mayhew,' I said aloud.

'Eulalia or — what was Sister Eulalia's name?'

'Before she entered the religious life?' Sister Bridget came back to stand beside me. 'She was Enid Fox, I think. When we take our vows we usually choose another Christian name with the same initial as our original name. It saves confusion. Now Sister Paul is really Pamela and Sister Felicity was — Fiona, I think. Me, I was always Bridget, though they called me Bridie at home.'

I looked for a moment longer at the two crosses and then turned away. There was nothing here that would shed light on Helen's death.

'Simon has undertaken to provide headstones for them as soon as the earth has settled,' said Sister Bridget as we walked away towards *Minstrel's Leap* again.

'He seems very generous,' I said.

'You must not think his teasing manner means a shallow heart. He has had more trouble than most in his life.'

'He gave *Minstrel's Leap* over to the Community, I believe?'

'That's true. His beautiful family home. The Shaws used to be very wealthy, I understand.'

'Used to be?'

The nun's rosy face flushed more vividly.

'I'm afraid Simon's father, the late Mr. Shaw, speculated rather unwisely,' she said in a faintly embarrassed tone. 'I ought not to have mentioned the fact. It really is none of my concern.'

'Mr. Shaw died three years ago, didn't he?'

'Such a sad accident. Of course he was not the only casualty. Two other people died and five were injured, including poor little Edith, of course.'

'What sort of accident was it?'

'A train crash. Didn't you read about it in the newspapers?'

'I was probably abroad at the time.'

'Ah, yes, with your father. It was a terrible affair.'

Quite unconsciously Sister Bridget had allowed a purely human note of excited horror to enter her voice.

'The train was derailed in the fog, just outside the station at York. Our convent was quite near, so we hurried over to do what we could. Thanks be to God, the loss of life was much less than it might have been. The train had slowed down because of the fog.'

'And Edith was on the train?'

'She was twelve years old. Ah, she had the prettiest face. Her father was taking her on a trip to York. He was killed at once, poor man.'

'And Edith? She was — ' I hesitated, not

sure how to phrase the question.

'We took her to the convent and looked after her until she was well enough to be moved,' Sister Bridget explained. 'Unhappily there was some brain damage. It slowed her down in some ways, made her more childish and it gave her headaches from time to time. She is sometimes a little quick-tempered.'

'I noticed that,' I said dryly.

'The specialist said that she will improve in time with care and a quiet life,' said Sister Bridget. 'But it's a great responsibility for Simon.'

'You met him at the time of the train crash?'

'Oh, yes, indeed.' She was chatting away freely now. 'We were able to identify Mr. Shaw from the documents in his pocket, and we notified his son. He came over the next evening, to see his sister and to arrange for his father's body to be brought back to *Minstrel's Leap*. After that, we became very friendly with him. Indeed, as you know, we all call him Simon now.'

'And two years later, he gave *Minstrel's Leap* to the Community.'

'Oh, there was nothing official about it,' she assured me. 'The house still belongs to the Shaws but we live there rent free. Simon insists that we're doing him a favour because the place was starting to deteriorate, but that's only his kindness. He might have sold the house at a profit.'

We had already reached *Minstrel's Leap*, but I wanted her to go on talking.

'You left York a year ago? May I ask why, Sister?'

'We had a very pretty house there,' she said, and her round face lengthened into regret. 'There was an orchard behind it and we were able to bottle pounds and pounds of apples and plums every year.'

'Then why did you leave?'

'The convent was burned down. It was in all the newspapers — oh, but I forgot, you would probably not have been in this country at the time. It was a terrible, terrible affair, but praise be to God, no lives were lost!'

'How did it happen? How did it start?'

'There had been a bonfire in the orchard that day,' Sister Bridget said. 'Sister Damian had raked together all the leaves and dead branches and we had a splendid bonfire. Edith enjoyed it so much. She jumped about, clapping her hands.'

'Edith was there?'

'Simon takes her over to York once or twice a year to see the specialist there. We were always pleased to see them.'

'And the bonfire? Was that how the fire started?'

'It had been left smouldering overnight. It was a safe distance from the house. We were all quite certain of that. During the night the wind must have risen. The bonfire rekindled and caught the wooden shed at the side of the convent. We used to store a lot of garden equipment there, and a lot of cleaning stuff, linseed oil and beeswax, things like that.'

'And the convent burned down?'

'There was barely time for us to get out of our cells,' Sister Bridget said. 'We lost everything. Even our chapel was completely gutted.'

'But nobody died.'

'We were all safe,' she said thankfully. 'We were so happy about that it didn't seem to matter that we were homeless, and as you see, it wasn't very long before we were rehoused at *Minstrel's Leap*.'

'Sister Eulalia? She joined you here?'

'We were expecting her round about the time the fire broke out,' Sister Bridget said. 'One of the Community had died a few weeks before, and Mother General had written to tell us about the new nun she was sending to replace Sister Teresa.'

'And how did Sister Teresa die?' I jerked out the question so abruptly that Sister

Bridget looked alarmed.

'Sister Teresa was nearly ninety years old,' she said at last. 'She died of old age, nothing more.' She gave me a sharp glance. 'Verona, child, now what kind of a question is that? What's in your mind?'

'Nothing,' I began, but her clear eyes impelled me. 'A year ago,' I said slowly, 'your convent at York burned down. And then a young Sister, who hasn't been with you for very long, catches a cold and dies of pneumonia. And then another Sister comes and, three weeks after she arrives, she falls over the rail of a high gallery.'

'In a Community, people do die from time to time!' Sister Bridget exclaimed. 'In every convent there are deaths. When I was a novice in Ireland we had four of the oldest Sisters all die within the space of a few months.'

'Sister Eulalia and Sister Hyacinth were not old ladies,' I said.

'Every convent also has periods of bad luck. Lack of money, a shortage of vocations — things like that often come together. There's no sense in letting your imagination run away with you,' she said, severely.

'Before the convent at York was burned down, was there anything else, Sister? Did anything else happen? Did any of the Sisters die?'

'Apart from old Sister Teresa? No, nobody. Nothing happened?'

I didn't know, but I was groping my way towards something. I could sense it, veiled, in the distance, but there was no way of lifting the veil.

'Ah, you're upset,' said Sister Bridget. 'It's easy sometimes to let your mind run away with you. It's not right to let it happen though. You must let the dead rest in peace.'

'Do they?' I asked fiercely. 'Do they rest in peace, Sister?'

'Glory be to God, of course they do!' She patted my arm several times. 'You must *not* brood about these things. We're a very happy Community. When you've stayed a week or two with us, you'll be finding your thoughts so silly! We live peacefully, child, and when bad things happen we pay the tribute of a little grief, and then we lift up our heads and go on again.'

It sounded simple. But I remembered the lines of strain in Mother Catherine's face, and Sister Felicity's hands, clutching the polishing cloth and rubbing furiously at the brass fender.

Something I had heard came into my mind so suddenly that I repeated it before I realized I had spoken.

'Felicity, Felicity,

Oh, such duplicity.'

Sister Bridget had paused and was looking at me in surprise.

'Now, fancy Sister Felicity repeating that to you!' she said. 'I really thought she was quite hurt about it at the time!'

'At the time?'

'When Sister Eulalia made it up,' she explained. 'At recreation one evening Sister Eulalia began to chant little verses about us — comic little verses for each one of us. She meant them to be amusing, I suppose, but some of them were a little — acid, you might say. Sister Elizabeth was quite cross about hers.'

'And Sister Felicity was hurt?'

'She was indeed, most unlike herself, for usually she's the first to see a little joke. I remember — '

'The verse? Was that all it was? Just those two lines?'

'I think so. 'Felicity, Felicity, oh such duplicity.' I can't remember anything more. Wait! There was another line, a third line.'

She furrowed her smooth brow.

'Try to remember,' I urged. 'Do please try to remember.'

'I do remember!' She snapped her fingers in triumph. ' 'Felicity, Felicity, oh such duplicity, Pills and potions, Herbs and lotions,' and oh yes! 'death a multiplicity.' That was it. Really an unkind little jingle. I was rather surprised at Sister Eulalia.'

'Felicity, Felicity,
Oh such duplicity,
Pills and Potions,
Herbs and Lotions,
Death a multiplicity.'

I repeated the words slowly. Then I asked, 'Sister, was Edith at your recreation that evening?'

'She was. The child often joins us if Simon has stayed on later than usual to lend a hand.'

'Sister Bridget, did you like Sister Eulalia?'

Taken by surprise she bit her lip and gave me an almost pleading look.

'We are supposed to love all our Sisters and we do in the spiritual sense, but it's not possible to *like* everybody equally. In human terms, that's not possible. And we none of us felt truly at ease with poor Sister Eulalia. She had a sharp tongue, a way of saying hurtful things while she was smiling. No, I'm bound to admit, she could be a little — difficult at times.'

8

As if conscious that she had been slightly indiscreet, Sister Bridget said nothing more and I had the sense not to press her. I was glad indeed, when the midday meal was over, to have the opportunity of being alone for a while, to consider everything I had learned.

Three years before, Mr. Shaw and his daughter, Edith, had taken a trip to York that had ended in tragedy with Mr. Shaw's death, and Edith subtly injured. After that nothing of any importance had happened for two years until the convent had been burned down and the nuns transferred to *Minstrel's Leap*.

It was here that Sister Eulalia had joined them, caught cold a year later and died of pneumonia within a week. And just over a week before I arrived at the guest house, Sister Hyacinth had fallen from the gallery and broken her neck.

And there were all the other little things that, taken singly might mean nothing at all, but added up to something that frightened me. Mother Catherine's strained face, Sister Felicity's clenched hands on the polishing rag, the malicious little verse invented by Sister Eulalia and repeated by Edith.

It was Edith, of course, who had been the mysterious voice whispering in my bedroom. No doubt she fancied herself as Lady Eadgyth.

Remembering that the door of my room had been bolted on the inside, I decided to examine every inch of the guest house.

But the splendour of the afternoon tempted me out of doors again. The moors blazed purple and gold under a blue sky across which tiny pink-edged clouds moved in dainty procession.

I took my sketching materials and went out to the back to continue with the drawing I had begun the previous day.

From where I sat I could look down towards Shaw's Cottage. It was of course necessary for me to sit in this particular position, because the house would appear in the finished painting.

Yet I found myself narrowing my eyes to bring into focus anybody who might be moving around near the white building, and I was furious with myself for the disappointment that welled up in me when nobody appeared.

It was stupid because I disliked Simon Shaw. Yet he was attractive and it might have proved amusing to quarrel with him if I had not had more urgent and important matters on my mind.

It was at that precise moment that he chose to come whistling around the corner of the yew hedge. I gave him a brief nod, to which he responded with a cheerful smile.

'Lovely day, Verona. Were you waiting for me?'

'It was lovely, and I'm not,' I said coldly.

'You know,' he regarded me amiably, 'at this rate we'll have used up all our quarrels before we get married and can look forward to a life of connubial bliss.'

'The joke's wearing thin,' I told him. 'It might have seemed amusing to you last night, but it's beginning to weary me. And for all you know I might be engaged already.'

'No rings,' he indicated. 'And I doubt if you have any secret understandings either.'

'How can you possibly know that?'

'You look sad when your face is in repose,' he told me. 'A face like yours ought to sparkle. It doesn't and that makes me wonder what happened to you.'

'My father died. He was my only relative.'

'A year ago, if I remember what you said last night. You must have been a devoted daughter to mourn for so long.'

'I was very fond of my father,' I said stiffly.

'Is that why you came up here?'

He lowered himself to the grass beside me.

'Sister Hyacinth used to be a friend of mine. I came because I read of her death in the newspaper.'

'You could have written to enquire about your friend,' he said.

It was true, of course. I had seized the opportunity to travel north, almost as if I were running away from myself. But it wasn't working out the way I'd planned. I had merely collected a host of new troubles without losing the memory of any of the old ones.

'I would like to know his name,' said Simon. 'I would like to know the name of the man who chased all the laughter out of your face. It would give me the greatest satisfaction to knock hell out of him!'

He spoke quietly and it was that quietness which made me believe him. Pierre had always spoken fast and fervently, a little more loudly than most men as if I were slightly deaf, and he'd had a habit of saying things twice over as if I were slightly stupid.

'It's none of your business,' I said, and felt tired as if all my love had drained out of me.

'No, of course it isn't, but one day you'll tell me because everything that concerns you interests me,' he said, and his glance was kind.

It mocked me again an instant later as he pointed to my drawing.

'I see I'm interrupting the fine flow of genius. That woman is still too big to fit inside the house, you know.'

'It's not a good drawing,' I said moodily. 'I was going to give it to the Sisters as a parting present, but it's useless.'

'The Sisters would be more interested in a painting of *Minstrel's Leap*,' he said. 'Or of the chapel. Now why don't you do one of the chapel?'

'I haven't seen it yet. Is it worth painting? I mean, would it make an interesting subject?'

'Come and see for yourself.'

Simon jumped up and held out his hand to me.

We went together through the gate and up the garden. Sister Damian was on her knees, weeding one of the vegetable beds. Simon paused briefly as we passed her.

'Will it be all right if I show the chapel to Verona?' he enquired.

'You know you're welcome in the chapel at any time, and have no need to ask,' she returned serenely.

'It's true, but I do have a certain feeling

that I shouldn't wear out my welcome,' he said in my ear.

In spite of myself I warmed towards this evidence of delicacy of feeling on his part.

We entered the door at the back of the hall and turned left towards the east wing. Simon dropped my hand and pushed open the door that led directly off the narrow lobby. The apartment beyond corresponded with the visitor's parlour in the west wing, and had been fitted up as a private chapel.

One glance set my fingers tingling to paint the walls, whitestoned and soaring, the elaborately carved and painted altar and ceiling, the clear sweep of the narrow pews, the light glowing redly below the frosted windows.

'The chapel was re-designed and decorated in the late seventeenth century,' Simon said. 'The nuns use it now, of course, but when I was a child my father used to have family prayers here. He was rather addicted to High Church ritual which greatly embarrassed the local minister.'

'It's perfect,' I said, in a low voice.

Indeed, the little chapel — it could not have held more than thirty people — was a harmony of light and shade, the gleam of silver and gold from altar and ceiling warming the white walls.

'There used to be more silver plate here,' Simon remarked. 'When my father began to lose money on the stock exchange he sold quite a lot of it.'

'What is above us?'

It had been from an upper window over the chapel that Edith had first looked out at me.

'A junkroom. Come up and take a look.'

He opened a low door at the side of the altar and beckoned me up winding stone stairs. We came out into a large, stonewalled room containing a variety of trunks and boxes.

'Edith comes here sometimes and dresses up.'

He pushed back the lid of a worn trunk and revealed a pile of dresses and hats pushed in an higgledy-piggledy fashion.

'These things belonged mainly to my mother and grandmother. The moth seems to have got at most of them.'

'Edith is very — fanciful,' I said awkwardly.

'She always had too much imagination,' he said shortly. 'Sometimes I think it would do her good to mix more with people of her own age. There's twelve years' difference in our ages, you know. But the nuns make a pet of her. Cousin Laura gets very cross at times for Edith spends more time up here than she does down at Shaw Cottage.'

'Do you allow the nuns to live here because they were kind to Edith after the accident?' I ventured.

'You heard about the accident then? Not from Cousin Laura, I'll be bound. She thinks that by never talking about it, she can convince herself that it didn't happen.'

'One of the Sisters mentioned it. She said you might have got a good price for it.'

'That's not true, I'm afraid.' He closed the lid of the trunk and gave me a rueful grin. 'The house is big and expensive to run. It's also isolated and the land hereabouts isn't rich enough to justify turning it into a farm. One could keep sheep, I suppose, but the profits would have to be ploughed back into the estate.'

'So you handed it over to the nuns?'

'Their convent at York burned down and it was the most practical thing to do. Shaw Cottage had been closed up ever since Cousin Laura's husband died, so we moved back there. The Sisters keep the house clean and aired, and they try to make an income in varying ways. I do what I can to help about the place. I'm not a wealthy man but we exist very comfortably.'

It sounded plausible but it had come out too smoothly. I watched him as he moved about the room, opening and closing the trunks and boxes, disturbing a fine layer of dust on some that were piled in the corner.

Had it been simply in gratitude that Simon had given up his home? I remembered what Sister Bridget had said that morning, about Edith clapping her hands in delight as the bonfire swirled high. Children loved flame and smoke and the crackling of twigs. And Edith was still part child, a spoilt child, a child who suffered from headaches and sudden outbursts of temper. Was it the guilty fear of what his sister might have done that had prompted Simon's generosity? Was that why he spent so much of his time at *Minstrel's Leap*? Not simply to help the nuns but to keep a close eye on Edith?

I asked, to distract the tenor of my thoughts, 'Are there any secret passages at *Minstrel's Leap*? In such an old house — ?'

'Were you hoping for oubliettes and underground tunnels thick with cobwebs? I'm afraid the Shaws have always been most prosaic. There's nothing at all, unless you count the concealed door at the back of the wardrobe.'

'One of the wardrobes in the guest house?'

'In the biggest room,' he nodded. 'There's a panel at the back that slides aside so that one can get into the next room. You have to know the right place to apply pressure before the thing opens.'

'Why was it made?'

'Not for any sinister reason,' Simon told me, looking amused. 'My great-grandfather thought, as you do, that such an old house needed a few secret cubbyholes. He had the panel put in, mainly so that he could play practical jokes on his house guests, I believe. He was what is politely termed a bit of an old rip.'

So that was how Edith had gone in and out of a room with a bolted door. I decided that I would block up the panel with something heavy before I went to bed. The tall firescreen could be jammed up inside the wardrobe and could create a beautiful clatter if the panel opened.

'What do you feel about making a picture of the chapel?' Simon enquired, opening the door and preparing to descend again.

'I'd like to do it,' I said. 'The painting would have to be oils. Nothing else is rich and flexible enough, but I could make some preliminary sketches inside the place. The focus would be the altar with the ceiling curved like a canopy about it and on each side of the foreground the kneeling figures of the Sisters, or perhaps their shadows cast in profile on the white walls. Oh, Simon, I'm sure I could make something beautiful!'

I got no further for he had turned below me on the stairs and his mouth was on a level with mine. And then my own mouth was pressed against it and I was sinking down into an embrace that was at once excitingly strange and sweetly familiar.

He let me go so abruptly that I almost fell down the remaining steps. I should have been angry. Later on I would be very angry, but at this precise moment I was limp with shock and with a treacherous pleasure that coursed along my nerves.

'I meant to take things a little more slowly,' he said. 'However it's probably as well that you realize how I feel.'

'But I don't — '

'But you're beginning to,' he interrupted. 'You know, it's quite fascinating, watching you wake up.'

'I was excited about the idea of painting the chapel. I can't neglect my art to get involved with people,' I stammered.

'I'm not people,' Simon said calmly. 'I'm the man who's going to marry you, and keep other people away so that you can get on with your art in peace, remember? Now, cast your eyes around again. Can't you see yourself all in white drifting up the aisle towards me?'

I could see myself only too plainly and my

eyes stung suddenly with tears. It would never happen. When Simon learned the truth he would never want to marry me. The insidious thought that he need never know entered my head, but my conscience rejected it. He ought to be told everything if I ever accepted his proposal and once told he would swiftly change his mind.

I averted my head slightly as I went through into the hall again. The Prioress was just emerging from her own quarters and she favoured me with her stately little bow.

'I've been showing Verona the chapel, Mother Catherine,' Simon said.

I caught a faint twitch of amusement in her face at his use of the Christian name.

'We always feel a little shy about taking visitors to the chapel. So many of them are terrified that we are planning to convert them! But it is a lovely chapel, don't you think?'

'I was hoping I might make an oil painting of it,' I said eagerly. 'I would give it to the Community as a gift, if it would be acceptable. I shall need to make sketches in the chapel, if that wouldn't be an imposition.'

'My dear, it would be a compliment,' Mother Catherine said warmly. 'But won't an oil painting take a very long time?'

'I said that I hoped to stay for about a month.'

'And you are still of the same mind? You find the guest house — pleasant?'

'Is there any reason why I shouldn't?'

'None.' She replied a trifle too quickly and her eyes were relieved.

'Sister Felicity has been spoiling me,' I said.

'She is an excellent nun,' said Mother Catherine. 'An excellent nun.'

She said it emphatically as if she expected to be contradicted, and a pulse beat at her smooth temple. Then she turned to Simon, and her tone was calm and business-like again.

'Could you grant me five minutes of your time?' she enquired. 'There are some returns on the vegetable profits that simply do not correlate with the expenses.'

'I'll come and play schoolmaster,' Simon said promptly.

'If you'll excuse me, please?'

Mother Catherine smiled as she bowed and moved away. Simon gave my shoulder a squeeze as he passed me. It was a 'See you later' gesture, but that was the one thing I was determined to prevent. It would be cruel and useless to allow a relationship to grow which was doomed to failure from the start.

As I returned to the garden I made up my

132

mind that I would concentrate upon two things for the rest of my stay. I would paint the finest oil study of which I was capable and I would find out why Helen had died.

If I met Simon again I would take care that it was in the company of others, and if the memory of his embrace troubled me then I would not dream at all.

Sister Damian was just finishing her weeding. She gave me a bright smile as I approached and surveyed her grimy hands ruefully.

'It's a constant wonder how I manage to get so dirty! Will you have a cup of tea with me in the kitchen, Miss Dean? I'm allowed to make one for myself when I've been hard at it.'

'Thank you, Sister, but please call me Verona.'

I opened the kitchen door for her and waited as she removed her heavy overshoes and put on a pair of light, heelless slippers, such as all the nuns wore indoors.

'Ah, I forgot. You mentioned the matter to Sister Bridget.'

Sister Damian waved me to a chair in the spotless kitchen and went over to the big stone sink to remove the canvas apron that protected her habit and to wash her hands.

'Sister Elizabeth is at her prayers,' she said

over her shoulder. 'She likes to have a quiet hour in the afternoon, because she is so busy most of the time that she sometimes has to fit in her devotions where she can. Now I am lucky, for in a garden one may pray fully and sincerely, without spoiling one's work.'

Her large brown eyes shone with the kind of joy usually reserved for a lover.

'Now we'll have a nice cup of tea,' she declared. 'Sister Elizabeth always leaves everything ready. Do you take milk and sugar? No? Then have a biscuit. You'll lose weight if you don't eat.'

Her own slim body swayed gracefully as she leaned over the table for cups and saucers. Sister Damian looked, I thought, like some exotic orchid transplanted to a kitchen garden and blooming there as happily as it had flourished in the tropics.

'I've been looking at the chapel,' I said, accepting my tea. 'It's an exquisite place.'

'It is!' She nodded enthusiastically. 'To be alone there is even better than being alone in a garden!'

'I thought I might make a painting of it while I'm staying here.'

'Are you an artist then? You know, I suspected that you might be, because of that big satchel you wear on your shoulder. And then we artists recognize each other.'

134

I was not at all sure that planting and weeding vegetable beds could compare with creating canvasses, but felt that she was entitled to her little bit of innocent vanity.

'Would it be possible for me to see some of your work some time?' she asked.

'You may see some now. They're unpolished, but it may give you an idea of my style.'

Unarmoured against the subtle flattery of her interest and trying to look as if I were used to requests from people to display my efforts, I gave her my two sketchpads and drank my tea with a fine assumption of indifference.

Sister Damian bent her veiled head and turned the pages, glancing up once or twice with an approving little nod.

'But you have great talent!' she exclaimed. 'I've seldom seen such lively — '

She stopped abruptly, her eyes downcast, but I could see the delicate colour fading from her pretty face. Then she closed the pad with a snap and rose, her eyes burning in her white face, her voice shaking.

'Please excuse me. I am not — oh, Miss Dean, how could you do such a wicked, such a spiteful thing? You are as bad as Sister Eulalia!'

9

Sheer surprise held me captive in my seat. The pad lay where she had flung it down on the table and after a moment I stretched out my hand towards it. The explanation for Sister Damian's astonishing outburst must lie in my drawings, but there seemed nothing at all in the assortment of half-completed scenes and lightly shaded faces that would cause such angry terror.

I was still puzzling over the drawings when Sister Paul came in. If she was surprised to find me in the kitchen, she gave no sign of it, but nodded pleasantly and helped herself to a cup of tea, with a small sigh which hinted that the lot of a novice was often a tiring one.

'Are you enjoying your holiday?' she asked me.

'Very much. I hoped to stay for two or three weeks longer.'

I answered her query with equal formal politeness, and eyed her thoughtfully, wondering how I could open the subject of Helen's death. She brought it up herself, however, sitting down opposite me, and regarding me gravely through her round spectacles.

'I'm sorry that Sister Hyacinth's death should have brought you here. It's a pity you were not able to visit her before.'

'Yes, indeed,' I said, rather guiltily, for it had never occurred to me even to enquire Helen's whereabouts. On an impulse I said, 'It seems inexplicable that she should have climbed up to the gallery.'

'I suppose she'd gone up to find the Minstrel,' said Sister Paul.

She gave the word a capital letter and ended with a breathless little giggle.

'The Minstrel?'

I spoke slowly, cautiously, not wanting to inhibit any confidences she was about to impart.

'He has been appearing for months,' Sister Paul breathed. 'Only we don't talk about it very much; but he's been seen, usually in the gallery and in the guest house.'

From the door behind me, Mother Marie said briskly, 'Sister Paul, have you no duties to attend?'

'Yes, Mother.' Scarlet to the rims of her spectacles, Sister Paul clattered down her barely tasted cup of tea and fled.

The Novice Mistress took the newly vacated chair and fixed me with a look in which acidity and humour were nicely balanced.

'I'm afraid it takes the full span of a novitiate before some of us learn discretion,' she observed.

'It was my fault. I was asking questions, to which I would still like to know the answers.'

She gazed for a moment at my uplifted chin as if she wished I were one of her novices so that she could scold me and send me about my duties.

'Sister Paul is young and inclined to indulge in romantic daydreaming,' she said. 'She has a vivid imagination.'

Mother Marie pronounced the word as if it were a rare and disfiguring rash.

'Did she imagine the Minstrel?'

I too gave the word a capital letter.

'That ridiculous story! Sometimes I wish I could meet that wretched Lady Eadgyth and give her a piece of my mind,' Mother Marie exclaimed. 'A sordid little intrigue with a down-at-heel musician, and a legend is born! All this nonsense about the minstrel haunting the gallery and the guest house.'

'But the guest house was not even built at that time!'

'Exactly, which shows what utter foolishness it is!' Mother Marie relaxed slightly. 'The house certainly has no tradition of haunting.

Simon assured us of that.'

'You found it necessary to ask him?'

'When we first came here and started the guest house there were two very pleasant ladies who came to stay. They actually intended to stay for three months; one of the ladies had been ill and needed a long rest. Unfortunately, within two weeks they made a very flimsy excuse and left. It was only after they left, when they wrote to thank us, that they mentioned having been alarmed during the night. It was all extremely vague and we had to take into consideration the fact that the lady had been suffering from a nervous complaint.'

'And was that all?'

'In the late autumn a family stayed here overnight. They were on their way to Scarborough, but made a detour because one of the children — there were two little girls — wanted to stay in a house where there were real live nuns.' She permitted herself a faint, wintry smile. 'They meant to stay only for a night or two. That was quite clear from the beginning, so there was no question of their leaving early.'

'Did something happen?'

'The younger girl evidently had a very disturbed night — nightmares and so on. It was all very vague.'

I considered for a moment whether or not to tell Mother Marie about Edith's attempt to frighten me, but some instinct held me back. What, after all, did I really know about any of these quiet women with their serene smiles and gentle voices? All of them had lives and characters of which I caught only occasional glimpses.

'Is it possible?' I asked hesitantly. 'Is it possible that Sister Hyacinth saw or thought she saw this Minstrel up in the gallery?'

'It is possible,' Mother Marie said doubtfully. She was obviously reluctant to admit that anything could have caused a nun to disobey a rule.

'In the excitement of the moment she might have forgotten that nobody was supposed to climb up to the gallery,' I said.

Some of the strain went out of the Novice Mistress's face and she shot me a glance that was almost benign.

'But you will not be leaving us for a while, will you?' she enquired after a few seconds. 'You are enjoying yourself in the guest house?'

'I haven't seen or heard any minstrels,' I said truthfully.

'And you are a sensible young woman,' she approved. 'I like to see good sense in a woman.'

I was uncomfortably silent, wondering if she would continue to regard me as sensible if I ever dared to tell her about myself and the events that had brought me back to England. Brought me running back, I amended my thought.

Mother Marie leaned forward slightly.

'Mother Catherine has told me that you're going to paint a picture of the interior of our chapel. May I say how wise you are to occupy your time with useful work? It never helps to brood.'

Did she guess that something more than concern for Helen's death troubled my mind?

'You must take some free time too,' she continued. 'Mrs. Cartwright has been very good to us since we came here, and of course we know Simon and Edith very well. It will do Edith the world of good to have a friend.'

She didn't mention Simon but I saw a matchmaking gleam in her eye and neatly side-stepped it by offering her my sketch-pad. I'm not certain what I expected after Sister Damian's outburst, but Mother Marie simply turned the pages looking closely at the sketches without comment.

'They're good,' she said at last. 'I think they're very good, but they have a bleakness about them. I hope you won't make the painting so bleak. There is no loneliness in the chapel.'

Somewhere a bell rang, sweet but insistent. The Novice Mistress rose at once, folding disciplined hands within her wide black sleeves.

'Prayers. Excuse me.'

She bowed slightly and went out at once. I stayed where I was for a few minutes, listening to the fading echoes of the bell.

It occurred to me that I might as well follow and try to get a rough plan of the chapel as the nuns knelt at prayer. The light was too bad by now to make more than a vague start but I wanted to begin. I was not willing to admit that in the dying light the kitchen seemed suddenly cold and gloomy.

Before I went to the chapel I would have another cup of tea. The thought of a hot drink was childishly soothing. The big teapot on the hob was still very pleasantly hot.

I lifted it carefully and poured a thin stream of amber liquid into my cup. It was more comfortable to stand by the glowing fire than to sit out in the centre of the room at the bare wooden table.

I sipped the tea and let my eyes rove slowly about the darkening walls. My shadow lay along the floor in the reddish gleam across the half-open door. The sun was setting and its last rays were cast over the garden.

I wished with all my heart suddenly that he would come in and find me and tell me how much he loved me. And I wasn't sure if it was Pierre or Simon who ran through my mind.

I clashed my cup impatiently into the sink, and was immediately visited by the fear that it might have cracked. A glance however reassured me. The crockery used by the nuns was thick and useful rather than decorative.

I wondered how long it had taken a woman like Mother Catherine to grow used to such inelegance. And Sister Damian who loved flowers and pictures — how often did Sister Damian crave bone-thin china and lace-edged tablecloths? I remembered how eagerly she had looked through my sketch book and then how she had snapped it shut, flinging it aside and crying out that I was worse than Sister Eulalia.

I wiped my hands on the towel that hung by the sink and picked up my sketching materials. The nuns would be deep into their worship now and unlikely to be disturbed if I slipped into the chapel.

I made my way through the refectory and the recreation room and turned aside into the chapel, pushing open the door cautiously lest the heavy wood creak.

Within, the white-washed walls reflected

the candles burning at the altar, contrasted with the kneeling black-robed figures. There was light enough for me to see by, and the measured responses of the Sisters made a soothing background against which lines and curves flowed out upon the white paper.

The focal point of the picture would be the altar, of course, the lines converging upon it, the nuns foreshortened but not exaggerated. Their veiled heads would be lifted up towards the altar and there would be candles suffusing the canvas in a gentle glow.

I knew of course that the vision in my mind would never attain absolute reality when it had been filtered through my hands, but if I could come close to the ideal then I would be satisfied. And that, I thought, with a little stab of pain, was why I would never be a genius but might possibly be happy again one day.

And then I was angry with myself because a year ago I would have sworn that my heart was broken and that there would be no more happiness for me.

The nuns were filing out now, their faces pale blurs within the darkness of their veils. It occurred to me then how easy it was for a woman to veil her personality within the austere habit of a nun. What did I know for certain about any of these women, beyond what they chose to reveal?

Sister Bridget had stayed to snuff out the candles, it being evidently her turn to perform this duty. The others would be sitting down to their supper now and it would be good manners for me to join them.

I closed my pad reluctantly, held by the beauty and the peace of the little chapel. Sister Bridget was kneeling now, the snuffer still in her hand, her face upturned to the dimly gleaming silver as if a sudden ecstasy had transfixed her there.

I was at the door, unwilling to trespass upon a private moment, when I heard her softly exclaim.

'Mother of God, who put that there?'

I went up and knelt beside her, looking up at the dark wood of the altar. It was then that I saw what had attracted her gaze. Half-masked by the thick candlestick, a little dark object leaned against the wood.

Sister Bridget rose and went up the two steps and took down the thing, holding it gingerly at arm's length.

'What is it, Sister?' My voice whispered in the silence beneath the half-extinguished candles.

She held it out to me, with disgust and bewilderment written plainly on her round face. I saw then that it was a doll, or to be more exact a crudely fashioned puppet of brown wood about six inches long.

It had been dressed in black serge roughly cut to suggest a religious habit and another piece of black material had been wrapped about the head. Some attempt had been made with white paint to delineate eyes, nose and mouth but what made the nasty little doll more horrible was the spike driven through its forehead. Driven with such force that the end of it protruded through the back of the wooden head.

'Who could have made such a dreadful thing?' Sister Bridget asked in a low voice. 'And to profane the altar with such an object! I shall have to take it to Reverend Mother.'

'Wait a moment!' I caught at her wide sleeve as she turned away. 'Come and sit down, please.'

'We'll be late for supper,' she hesitated, but allowed me to lead her to one of the pews.

'Was that — thing on the altar when you all came in to prayers?' I asked.

'It was not.' Her answer was prompt. I must have looked surprised for she said in explanation, 'It is my turn to light the candles and prepare the altar this week. We all take it in turns, except for Sister Elizabeth, of course. She is excused from evening prayers because she has our supper to get ready. I came in to light the candles and to lay down the hassocks. There was nothing on the altar then.'

'You couldn't possibly have missed it?'

'I could not.'

'Then it was placed on the altar during prayers. I came in later than the rest of you and I never saw anyone move until it was time to leave.'

'What are you saying?' she asked, and there was fear in her face.

'Before I came in, did any of you have occasion to go up to the altar?' I enquired.

'We all had occasion to go up to the altar,' she said in a low voice and all the merriment had died out of her face as if it had never been. 'We come in one by one, not in any particular order, and we go up to the altar and kiss the Holy Bible before we take our seats.'

'Where is the Bible kept?'

But I had seen it, on a ledge at the right of the altar, just below the candlesticks. Anyone, bending to kiss the heavily tooled volume, could have stretched up slightly and laid the puppet down on the dark wood. Anybody could have done it, and those who followed need not have noticed anything.

'Do you always sit in the same places?' I asked.

Sister Bridget shook her head.

'In chapel we are all equal in the sight of God,' she said, 'and we kneel wherever we choose.'

'And never notice where the others sit?'

'We are in the chapel to pray,' she said, faintly reproving, 'not to notice who sits where.'

'So anyone in the Community could have put that on the altar,' I said slowly.

'Child, what are you saying? Nobody could have done such a horrible, such a blasphemous thing!'

Her eyes were enormous within the white coif.

'It didn't walk there,' I said.

'But, whoever made this must hate us,' she said in a bereft, childish voice. 'We are a happy Community. Believe me, we are a happy Community!'

'Somebody put the doll there,' I repeated.

Her small hand reached out and took the doll back, as she rose with a decision in her bearing that gave her a touching dignity.

'I will take this to Mother Catherine at once,' she said. 'Will you come in to supper now? We are very late, very late indeed. I shall have to do penance.'

'I'm not very hungry,' I said truthfully. 'Would you tell Mother Catherine that I'm going to my room. There'll be biscuits and lemonade there and I can only manage a light snack anyway.'

'I shall give the thing to Mother Catherine after supper,' Sister Bridget said. 'The others will be at recreation and I will have to go to the parlour to be scolded.'

She gave me a gallant, shaky little smile and genuflected solemnly. Half the candles on the altar were still alight and she was evidently too perturbed to remember them. So I took up the snuffer she had laid down, and put out the candles, and hurried away from the dark chapel through the echoing hall and to the comparative cheer of the guest house.

The lamps were lit and the fire crackled invitingly. It gave me a sense of security to know myself locked in, with the key in my pocket and the windows closed against the night.

I checked that the firescreen was in place at the back of my wardrobe. If Edith took it into her head to play Lady Eadgyth the resulting clatter as she slid aside the false back would wake the soundest sleeper.

As I drank lemonade and munched biscuits I went on thinking about pretty, silly young Edith. It was easier to think of her pranks than it was to allow my deeper foreboding to take charge of my imagination. But sooner or later I would have to take my fears out into the light of day where I hoped they would shrivel up and die.

But they would not die nor shrink into the limbo of unimportant things. The convent at York had been burned down. Sister Eulalia had died suddenly of pneumonia. Sister Hyacinth had fallen from the gallery. Somebody had driven a spike through the head of a puppet dressed as a nun.

Those events could not be explained away. They were facts, linked by the presence of Edith. Pretty Edith with her long red hair and sweet voice, who frightened guests away from the convent and dressed up as Lady Eadgyth waiting for the minstrel. Was that the limit of her activities or did she go beyond play-acting and practical jokes?

My compassion at the instant was not for the nuns, but for poor Simon who loved and protected his young sister. I sensed that his feelings for Edith were bound up with gratitude to the nuns who had cared for her after the train crash. Gratitude and guilt because he knew Edith had caused the fire? But surely, knowing that, he would never allow her to wander about freely.

I shook away thoughts of Simon and picked up my sketch book, seeking to divert myself with another look through the pages.

The last sketch, the one I had done in the chapel, pleased me. Allowing for the poor quality of the light the balance of the composition was good.

The altar reared up to the top of the page and below it the black shapes of the Sisters yearned towards it. Eleven black smudges, their hidden faces raised to the candles. But that was wrong. I had made a mistake because there had been only ten nuns in chapel.

Sister Elizabeth was excused from evening prayers because she had the supper to cook. Sister Bridget had said that distinctly. But in the sketch there were eleven tiny black blobs!

Either she had made a mistake or another figure robed in black had joined the nuns, had filed into the chapel, had kissed the great Bible at the side of the altar and had left quietly when the others did, head bent beneath the veil, hands folded within the wide sleeves, and in her heart an evil and twisted glee, the insane merriment of a child with a sick mind.

10

I was crossing the hall the next morning when the door leading to the parlour opened and the Prioress beckoned me inside. Pale and dignified as ever, yet it was obvious from the heaviness of her lids that she had slept badly.

'I understand that you were in the chapel when Sister Bridget found the effigy,' she said, coming to the point at once with no morning greeting.

'I remained behind to furnish my preliminary sketch.' I said.

'I received a vague impression of somebody sitting near the back. Sister Bridget brought the thing to me during recreation,' she said thoughtfully. 'She assures me that it was not on the altar at the beginning of prayers. That can only mean it was placed there during our prayers. I have not yet mentioned this to any of the others.'

She paused, looking at me, and I said quickly and reassuringly, 'Believe me I will say nothing.'

'It is so impossible to imagine any of the Community could be responsible,' she said.

'It need not have been.'

Hoping to relieve her mind a little I told her how I had sketched eleven figures, when only ten should have been present. She seemed unconvinced however.

'You were expecting eleven of us to be present, so you may have added the extra figure because you had the final composition in your mind. And where would this extra figure come from? How would it obtain a habit?'

'May I ask how many habits the nuns possess?'

'Two each,' she said promptly. 'Every three months the outer habits are washed and ironed and a clean one given out. Those that have been washed are stored in my own cell and given out again when the three months are up. And I keep the key to the cupboard myself.'

'Then nobody could have taken one of the spare habits.'

'Who would wish to do such a thing?'

I swallowed and ventured the name, but Mother Catherine shook her head.

'Edith is, as you evidently know, a trifle retarded as a result of the injuries she suffered in the train crash,' she said. 'She likes to come here and dress up as the lady of the manor. We know that and let her alone, for it amuses her and does no harm. But she would never do anything to hurt or frighten us.'

It was on the tip of my tongue to tell her about my first night in the guest house when I had been almost frightened out of my wits, but the Prioress had moved towards the door again.

'I have bound Sister Bridget to secrecy,' she said. 'I would be grateful for the same pledge from yourself. This is my responsibility.'

'And the puppet?'

'I burned it,' she said. 'Fire can be cleansing, you know. But, of course, it cannot end there. I am the Prioress here and responsible for the spiritual and physical welfare of the Community. If one of my nuns is so disturbed that she is driven to acts of blasphemy, then it is for me to discover it, else I will have failed.'

It seemed strange to me that the Prioress had dismissed any notion of Edith's being responsible, preferring instead to believe that one of her own nuns had been guilty of the sinister, malicious action. That could only mean that the Prioress suspected that someone in the Community was capable of such a deed.

Presumably the Prioress would know the background histories of the Sisters. She would know the names they had used in the world, something of their families.

I knew only that Sister Hyacinth had been Helen Mayhew, and Sister Eulalia had been Enid Fox — and both were dead. Sister Bridget had been Bridie at home in Ireland. But I knew nothing about any of the others, not even about Mother Catherine herself.

Deciding that speculation was addling my brain and leading me into the realms of fantasy, I mentally shook myself and went on into the chapel whose beauty, even in pale daylight, pleased my eyes and set my fingers itching with the desire to recreate it in swathes of brown and white, black and silver and the yellow of thin candle flames.

I worked hard for the rest of the morning and went out after lunch for a walk, to stretch my legs a little and draw the clean, moorland air into my lungs. I had hoped to see Simon, but the first person I met was Edith, climbing the slope towards me with a great basket on her arm.

'Whinberries!' she said gaily, showing me the contents. 'It's late to be picking them but the crop was so good this year and lasted so long! I shall take them up to the kitchen and Sister Elizabeth will let me help her to make pies.'

'You're very fond of the Sisters, aren't you?' I ventured.

'I know a lot about them,' she said with a childish slyness in voice and face. 'They talk to me. Did you know that Sister Elizabeth was engaged to be married once? But on the day before the wedding the young man went off and married another lady. And Sister Paul wanted to be a writer, but she didn't have any talent for it, or for anything else either, so she went into a convent.'

It sounded an unlikely reason for anyone taking the veil, and I said so. But Edith laughed, fingering her lips, and skipped on to another subject.

'It was good of you not to tell Cousin Laura that you'd seen me at the window above the chapel,' she said. 'She gets very cross if I go up too often.'

'Perhaps she thinks you disturb the nuns,' I suggested.

'Well, why shouldn't I?' she demanded, all the good temper wiped from her face. 'Why shouldn't I go to *Minstrel's Leap*? It belonged to the Shaws, before my brother gave it to the nuns. And it was *my* home too, but nobody asked me how *I* felt about it!'

I opened my mouth to argue, but she pushed the basket into my hands.

'I've changed my mind,' she said rudely. 'You can carry these to Sister Elizabeth yourself!'

She had turned away and was running back towards the little white house. I stood watching her, remembering that I had not received a return invitation nor seen Simon at all that day. Not that it mattered, I told myself.

Simon had evidently come to the age when he had decided he needed a wife, and he had been sufficiently attracted to fix his choice upon me. But when he knew about my father and about Pierre, he would quickly change his mind.

I bit down on the treacherous thought that he need never know about the events of that last summer in Paris. I could never marry a man who knew nothing about me. And, realizing that I had begun to think about Simon Shaw as a prospective husband, I sternly forbade myself to think about him at all and took the whinberries back to Sister Elizabeth.

It rained over the weekend, soaking down upon the moor and the garden, making it necessary for lamps and fires to be lit most of the day. On Sunday a small, round priest, wrapped in oilskins, dismounted from a dripping pony and was ushered in to hear confessions, and to offer Mass. I caught a glimpse of him, being fussed over by the Sisters, and bolted to my room, having the uneasy feeling that I might be expected to attend the service.

The few days passed slowly but not unpleasantly. Yet I was aware of a restlessness in myself as if it were spring and my heart was gentle again, and not scarred by flames leaping to the sky, and a door closed in my face, and the scent of chestnut blossom under my feet.

When I probed my own unhappiness I was conscious of a dull ache, as if the raw wound were healing. And I wanted to see Simon again, to listen to his voice that mocked and caressed me at the same time, and see his warm smile and puckered eyebrow when he studied one of my drawings.

Very soon, if I didn't keep a close guard on myself, that girl in the drawing would be small enough to fit into the little house.

On Monday the rain ceased and everything looked newly-washed. The grass was an impossible green against a blue-white sky, and a web of dew was spread over the kitchen garden, and glittered as if each drop contained every colour of the rainbow.

I coiled my hair over my ears and craved small red roses to fasten in the loops. And then I scolded myself severely for allowing my thoughts to wander when I ought to have been concentrating on the problem that had brought me up to Yorkshire in the first place.

Helen who had been my friend was dead, and I was here — I stopped at this point, or tried to stop, but the words ran on in my mind. I was here to find out who had pushed Helen over the low rail to the gallery.

I picked up my sketching book and went out into the hall. I had completed the preliminary studies for the chapel and ought to be setting up my easel, but the sunshine beckoned me. It was that and not the hope of meeting Simon, I told myself, that sent me out on to the moor.

Evidently others had had the same idea. I caught a glimpse of little Sister Paul trotting off in the direction of the village and for a moment was tempted to call after her to wait for me. I had not yet been into the village.

Another black-robed figure was disappearing around the corner of the building. I recognized the tall, erect bearing of the Novice Mistress. She was striding out as if she enjoyed the sensation of moving over the wet grass.

'Good morning. I see you've decided to take advantage of the altered weather.'

The Prioress had come out, and was standing on the steps behind me.

'I thought I'd go for a walk.'

I felt absurdly guilty as if I were one of the

novices dodging some duty or other.

'Sister Paul is going for a walk too. Today is her birthday and she is accordingly excused many of her duties.'

'I suppose you know the birthdays of all the Sisters?'

'Most of us are at an age when we prefer to forget them,' she said permitting herself a small smile. Then, the smile fading as if she had read my thoughts, she said, 'Of course I know everything about my nuns. It is necessary for me to do so, but it is not necessary for the other Sisters to know everything about their companions. We are not forbidden to talk about our former lives, you understand, but it is not encouraged.'

'But if one of the Sisters is — *ill*?'

'I know each one of my nuns,' she said frostily. 'I can assure you that if one of them is discovered to be — ill, as you phrase it, then I shall take the customary steps.'

'But this isn't a customary situation,' I burst out. 'Mother Catherine, surely you can see — '

'I can see that you are still upset and worried over the death of your friend,' she said a shade more kindly, 'but you must not allow your imagination to run away with you.'

She gave me a brisk, dismissing nod and went back into the hall. If she longed to drop her duties and wander out into the fresh air, not a muscle of her calm face had betrayed it. I envied her such self-discipline, and envied her the more as I saw Simon coming towards me, for colour surged into my cheeks and I could not prevent a delighted smile from lifting the corners of my mouth.

'I went over to York on business,' he greeted me. 'Did you think about me over the past few days?'

'Not at all,' I said stiffly.

'How charmingly you lie! Pretty women should tell lies more often, it imparts a becoming sparkle to the eyes, and a twitch to the lips.'

'I thought of you occasionally,' I admitted, and the colour ebbed from my cheeks so that I felt suddenly vulnerable.

'And I never stopped thinking of you.' He drew my hand through his arm and gave me his attractive, disturbing grin. 'How is the painting going?'

'I haven't even begun,' I confessed.

'Will you be able to paint in the chapel? Is the light good enough there?'

'Mother Catherine has given me permission to leave the door of the chapel open when I set up my easel there, but I can do a lot of it from memory, and I've made several sketches.'

We were walking across the grass, and it was pleasant to be close to him and talking with him.

'You didn't ask me why I went to York,' he said.

'I heard you say that you went on business. I assumed it was your own.'

'I hope to make my business yours,' he said gravely. 'I went to York to consult a doctor.'

'Are you sick?'

I must have clutched at his arm, for he looked pleased at my anxiety but shook his head.

'I went to see a doctor about my sister, about Edith,' he told me. 'I've never given up hope that one day she will be completely cured. Whenever I hear of a new physician, a new theory, then I follow it up.'

'Did you take Edith with you?'

'I left her in Cousin Laura's charge. I went up myself to talk to the doctor first, but it was another blind alley.' There was sadness in his face and he said, violently as if he had forgotten I was there and was talking to himself, 'Edith has been through enough; has suffered enough. I'll not expose her to every charlatan who comes along flourishing a medical degree.'

We paced in silence for a few yards.

'I'm sorry,' he said. 'I didn't intend to share

only troubles with you. I would like to share everything. I've wanted to, ever since I saw you getting off the train at the level crossing, with that ridiculous trunk and an exceedingly cross expression on your face.'

'You don't know me,' I stammered.

'I knew, as soon as I saw you, that I wanted to marry you,' Simon said. 'I knew it as surely as if a voice had said to me, 'This is the girl you're going to love.' Wasn't it like that for you too?'

I wanted to tell him then. I wanted to shout out, 'Yes, it was exactly like that for me. But not here, not in this quiet, green place. In Paris, a year ago, it happened to me. The chestnut trees were all blossom and the air was sweet with the perfume of crushed petals. And a dark young man came out of a café and smiled at me. And I was mistaken at that time, mistaking dross for gold, and the sparkle of glass for the brilliance of a diamond. And I told myself, when it was all over, that it could never happen to me again, that I would never let it happen.'

'Come to supper again soon,' he urged. 'Come tomorrow evening. I want you to get to know Edith better; and Cousin Laura. They would be delighted if I took a wife.'

'So you are only marrying in order to oblige your Cousin Laura,' I said.

It was best to keep the tone of the conversation light and teasing. He was sensitive enough to humour my mood at once, relaxing his pressure on my arm.

'Not at all,' he said solemnly. 'I intend marrying you so that I can fill up the spaces on the walls with pretty pictures.'

'Good morning, Simon. Isn't it a beautiful day? You went out so early that I had no chance to cook you a proper breakfast!'

Laura Cartwright blocked our path, having approached without our noticing. There was an appreciative twinkle in her eyes, as if she guessed that we had been absorbed in each other.

'I drove the Sisters over to school early,' he said. 'They wanted to get their pupils dressed up and the best work put out on show, ready for some school inspection or other. I'm sorry, I should have told you.'

'Simon is so very kind,' Laura said to me, rather as if she were supplying him with a testimonial. 'He helps the Sisters in every way he can, and they, in turn, help us with their prayers.'

'I've invited Verona to have supper with us tomorrow night,' Simon said.

'Edith will be so pleased!' Laura clapped her hands. 'She has taken a real fancy to you, my dear.'

'Has she?' I tried to sound pleased instead of sceptical.

'Perhaps you would bring some of your sketches over,' she went on. 'I was always considered rather artistic when I was a girl.'

'I'd be very glad,' I said politely.

'Are you on your way to the convent?' Simon asked.

'I was looking for Edith,' Laura said. 'The naughty girl slipped out of the house and ran off. I thought she might have come bothering the nuns again.'

'They don't mind. Mother Catherine told me so,' I said.

'They say that they don't, but it can't be pleasant for them to be continually inter-rupted,' Laura said repressively. 'I did hope she might have simply taken a stroll, but I only met two of the nuns on their way to put some flowers on the grave of that poor one who died.'

'I'd better look for Edith,' Simon said, sounding resigned.

I had the feeling that he sometimes grew a little tired of Laura's fussing. He withdrew his arm from mine with obvious reluctance and gave me a warm smile that made my heart turn over again with a mingling of pain and pleasure.

I walked on aimlessly for a while, but with

nobody to talk to some of the glow had gone out of the morning. And yet I must guard my tongue when I was with him. I must take care never to mention Pierre or my father, because it would hurt me too much to rip open the wound. I must not mention my suspicions about Edith, either, because that would hurt him, and I was already sufficiently involved with him not to wish to cause him any pain.

I went back around the side of the house into the garden. Sister Damian was there, gardening boots and gloves and a canvas overall concealing her habit, but failing to detract from the exquisite, almost luminous beauty of her features. She gave me a swift, half-fearful glance and bent over the spade again, but I stepped up and gave her a clear and cheerful good morning.

'Good morning, Miss Dean.' Her voice sought to be cool but trembled.

'I'm afraid my drawings upset you the other day, Sister. It wasn't intentional,' I said, awkward with sympathy.

'I was not feeling quite myself,' she said stiffly.

'If there is anything I can do — ' I began, but she put up her hand as if to ward me off.

'There is nothing, truly. Nothing that you or anybody else can do. It would oblige me if you would simply put my stupidity right out of your mind.'

I nodded, uncomprehending, but touched by her air of desperation. She had gone back to her digging, striking the spade feverishly into the heavy earth as if she were trying to bury some terrible personal trouble. I wanted to help, but I had no right to pry into her business, so I went back into the chapel where I set up my easel and, with the door propped open, made a determined and concentrated start upon the painting.

When I am working, hours telescope into minutes, and the real world becomes cloudy and unimportant. So I painted steadily, immersed in colour, until the colour began to fade and the air to darken into late afternoon.

'We have prepared something for you to eat in the kitchen. You didn't hear the dinner bell,' Sister Elizabeth said at my shoulder.

'I'm sorry, but I was immersed in my work,' I apologized.

'We didn't wish to disturb you, but a nice cup of tea and some cake might not come amiss?'

'I am hungry,' I said and realized it was true. 'Will the easel be in the way here?'

'Not at all,' she assured me. 'But do come along now, or the tea will be stewed. Sister

Paul will keep you company as soon as she returns.'

'Is Sister Paul out?' I remembered as I spoke that I had seen her that morning.

'She went for a walk.'

'Of course, because it's her birthday. Mother Catherine told me.'

'Birthday or not, she's no business to go taking the entire day off,' Sister Elizabeth said, with a touch of asperity. 'Sister Paul is not yet fully professed and ought not to abuse her privileges. Mother Marie will be very cross.'

'But surely Sister Paul came back for dinner!' I exclaimed.

'That she did not!' said Sister Elizabeth. 'Out she goes for her birthday ramble, and out she stays.'

'But it's getting dark.'

A prickle of fear touched the base of my spine.

'And it's going to rain again if I'm any judge. I only hope she had the sense to put on her boots,' Sister Elizabeth said.

The prickle of fear was hardening now into premonition.

11

While I was drinking my tea, Sister Bridget and Sister Marguerite arrived from the inspection day at school.

'Holy Mother of God, but I never met a schools' inspector before, and I hope I never shall again!' Sister Bridget exclaimed as she came through the kitchen door. 'He was poking around in every cupboard and asking more silly questions than you'd hear in a month of Sundays! Have you a spare cup of tea for Simon? He's carried up the new sewing baskets, and he deserves a cup!'

I drank my own cup which tasted suddenly scalding for the colour flooded my face as he came in.

'Good evening, Sister Elizabeth.' He gave her a slight bow and lifted an eyebrow in my direction. 'Verona, good evening.'

'Where did you put the baskets?' Sister Elizabeth asked, handing him a cup.

'Just inside the hall. Sister Joan is dealing with them.'

'Did you find your sister?' I had controlled my face and voice.

'Lord, yes. The silly girl had taken it into

her head to go off looking for wild flowers, but there's not much beyond heather and harebells.'

'Did you happen to meet Sister Paul on your way?' Sister Elizabeth asked.

'But surely it's Sister Paul's free day,' Sister Marguerite said.

'Within reason. She's not free to go jaunting off all by herself, with never a word as to when she's coming back,' Sister Elizabeth said crossly.

'Is there any place she's likely to have gone?' Simon enquired.

'Bird watching,' Sister Marguerite said promptly. 'Sister Paul has always been interested in birds. You remember how upset she was when Sister Damian put lengths of cotton over the peas.'

'She'd hardly be watching birds at this hour,' Sister Bridget objected, 'unless she has a passion for owls.'

The three nuns looked at one another uneasily. The panes of the kitchen window were quite black now, and there was a spatter of rain against the glass.

'I'll take the pony-trap and have a look around,' Simon said. 'We'll probably find Sister Paul on her way home. Verona, will you come with me?'

'You'd better borrow my oilskin cape,'

Sister Elizabeth said briskly, reaching up to the hook behind the door.

'You don't think anything could have — happened to Sister Paul, do you?' whispered Sister Marguerite.

'I think it's highly unlikely,' Simon said easily. 'Give us an hour and we'll come back to report. And it wouldn't hurt to have a look inside the house. She may have returned already.'

But I noticed that he took my arm and shepherded me through the door without waiting for the result of the search, and hurried me through the garden and round the side to where the pony-trap stood. Beyond the sheltering walls the wind blew gusts of rain into our faces.

'Do you think something *has* happened to Sister Paul?' I asked, as he helped me up to the seat.

'I doubt it,' he said, 'but it's not usual for the Sisters to wander off by themselves all day. What bothers me is that somebody called at our place yesterday making enquiries about nuns.'

'Who was it?'

'I never saw him myself. I was soaking off the grime of York in a hot bath. Cousin Laura opened the door.'

'But who was he? What did he want?'

'He was dark-haired, youngish, and spoke with an accent. French, Laura thought.'

I must have made some involuntary movement, for he broke off and I saw him glance at me in a puzzled fashion.

'He didn't give his name,' he continued, 'so Laura didn't invite him inside. She said he asked if there was a convent belonging to the Daughters of Compassion in the district. When she said there was he spun some story of having a cousin in the Order — a very pretty, dark-haired girl, he said.'

I was cold from more than the wind and the rain. A dark-haired Frenchman seeking a pretty girl — it must be, could only be Pierre. A few months ago the idea that he might be in the neighbourhood would have roused in me a trembling hope. Now I was consumed by an icy fear, lest he discover me and try to open again what had been finished.

Finished? As the word came into my mind my terror was succeeded by an immense and infinite relief. I might never be able to accept what Simon offered, but at least I was free of Pierre. Free of him, even though he had come looking for me.

'Cousin Laura was not impressed by the gentleman's manner, though one has to make allowances for the fact that she distrusts every foreigner on principle,' Simon said. 'But it did strike me as odd.'

'Did you mention it to Mother Catherine?' I asked.

'I didn't know about it myself until Cousin Laura told me this morning. You remember, we met her when she was running round in circles looking for Edith.'

'So she was afraid your sister might have met this foreigner?'

'Something like that.' He raised his voice slightly above the wind. 'But I'd back Edith any day. She may look as frail as a reed, but she's more like coiled steel, especially when she gets into a temper. We'd better shout for Sister Paul, don't you think? We'll never see her in all this.'

We raised our voices into the wind, and the wind caught them and flung them back into our faces. No voice was lifted in reply, and nothing met my straining gaze but the dark billows of grass through which the pony trotted, and the grotesque curve of cloud and sky glimpsed dimly through the rain.

'This is useless,' Simon said at last, impatience edging his tone. 'It's obvious she's not within hailing distance.'

'She might be lying hurt.'

'It's possible she slipped and twisted her ankle,' he agreed. 'She may have been caught

173

in a snare. I don't set them myself, but the local lads occasionally do. However, being a natural optimist, I prefer to believe she's safely indoors by now. So dinna fash thysen, wench!'

His sudden descent into the vernacular was meant to make me laugh, but tears filled my eyes and mingled with the rain on my cheeks, so that I was glad of the darkness.

As we drew up at the main door of the convent it opened and the tall figure of Mother Marie beckoned us within.

'Come into the parlour and take off your wet things,' she said. 'I assume you have not found Sister Paul? Well, she is certainly not in the house.'

'You're certain of that?' Simon said.

'Quite certain. We even looked in the guest house, though there is no reason why Sister Paul should go there. It will be necessary to launch a search.'

'I'll go down to the village and get some of the men.'

Simon, having assisted me from the pony-trap, climbed back into his seat.

'We intend to light lanterns and search ourselves, in pairs,' Mother Marie said firmly. 'It is better than staying here, doing nothing.'

'I'll get down to the village then.'

He slapped the reins across the pony's back

and it set off at a spanking pace, dreaming no doubt of a warm stable and dry hay.

'Come inside, child, and dry yourself.'

Mother Marie was stripping off the oilskin and hurrying me into the parlour. Mother Catherine was there, fine lines of strain etched on her face.

'My dear, it was very good of you to venture out,' she said. 'The others Sisters are just finishing their supper and then they will set out in pairs to look for Sister Paul.'

'Simon has gone to the village to raise a search party,' Mother Marie said.

'Simon is kind as always,' the Prioress nodded. 'Now, Mother, I suggest that you go with Sister Anne. We cannot run the risk of mislaying another novice.'

'Certainly, Mother Catherine.'

'I will accompany Sister Marguerite, and Sister Bridget had better go with Sister Joan. Sister Damian and Sister Perpetua can go together.'

'Which leaves Sister Felicity.'

'Who will remain here. We cannot leave the convent unattended. And Sister Felicity's nursing experience may be useful.'

Unbidden, the rhyme popped into my mind.

Felicity, Felicity,
Oh, such duplicity.
Pills and potions,
Herbs and lotions,
Death a multiplicity.

Sister Eulalia had made up the rhyme but Sister Felicity had not borne any grudge. She had nursed Sister Eulalia through the cold that had turned so unexpectedly to pneumonia, but Sister Eulalia had died all the same.

'Shall I come out with you again?' I offered, but my voice must have sounded weary, for both the nuns shook their heads.

'We have no right to expect it of you, but if you could stay up for a few hours? Sister Felicity might be grateful for some company later. But do feel free to use the parlour, and help yourself to whatever you need. You haven't had supper yet, but Sister Elizabeth was rather upset and we made do with cold meat and salad.'

They bowed and went out together, two dignified women hiding their fear under a gentle and determined discipline.

I warmed my hands at the fire, but the rest of me was chilled to the bone. Through the half-open door I could hear low voices and glimpse the flickering of lanterns.

A little while later there was silence, save

for the crackling of wood in the hearth. I might have been alone in the house, but I knew that Sister Felicity was somewhere about, probably in the kitchen. I was not sure if the knowledge reassured me or not.

I realized that I was, by now, extremely hungry. There would be food in the refectory if it hadn't been cleared away.

I opened the parlour door more widely and went out into the great, echoing hall. It stretched up into infinity and out to immensity, and it was dark, save for a faint glow from the chapel.

I went towards that glow, noting the chapel door was ajar. I pushed it wider and saw Sister Felicity kneeling before the altar, her face hidden in her hands. It would have been tactless to intrude upon her petition, so I went back into the ante-room and thence through the recreation rooms to the refectory.

A lamp burned here and the remains of a meal was on the table. I sat down in my customary place and helped myself to meat and some of the brown bread and butter. The silence pressed round me. The reading of a psalm would have been preferable to the quietness.

'My dear, I'm so sorry not to have been here to serve the meal.'

Sister Felicity's voice made me jump.

'I shall have to do penance. I'm late for supper,' I said, and she was kind enough to laugh a little at my foolish joke.

'Sister Paul will have to do a great deal of penance when she returns,' she said, but her voice broke on the last word.

'I'd love a cup of coffee, Sister,' I said quickly.

'I'll get you one at once. Shall we have one together in the kitchen? It's good to keep busy,' she said promptly.

I followed her into the kitchen where a fire burned brightly and a number of candles had been lit. It was warm and cheerful and Sister Felicity bustled about efficiently.

'It's obvious that you were a nurse,' I said, but the effect of my words was quite different from what I had intended. Her face went so pale that it gleamed sickly-green and her hand shook so violently that most of the coffee slopped over into the saucer.

'Who told you?' she asked sharply. 'Who told you that I had been a nurse? Not Mother Catherine? She would never tell anybody.'

'Sister Eulalia knew.' I wasn't sure what I was talking about but I knew it was important. 'She made a rhyme up about it. She knew.'

'Why wouldn't she know?' Sister Felicity asked bitterly. 'Enid Fox's father was one of the finest journalists of his day. He covered the trial.'

'The trial; yes.'

I nodded, trying to look understanding, but Sister Felicity had lost her reticence, partly through the stress of her present anxiety, partly because she thought I knew her story already.

'Fifteen years,' she said slowly, 'and it haunts me still. I tried so hard, you know, to be a good nurse. And I made Mrs. Carson happy and comfortable because I liked her. I never dreamed that she would leave me any of her money. They said that I'd wheedled my way into her affections and then withheld her medicine deliberately, but it wasn't like that.'

'No, of course not.'

'I'd been awake for two nights. I couldn't keep my eyes open a moment longer. And Mrs. Carson had another attack and tried to reach the bottle instead of ringing the bell. The bottle must have been knocked off the table when she fell. But I didn't break it myself. The jury believed me in the end, of course.'

'It was a long time ago,' I said helplessly.

'I gave away the money to charity, and I entered the Order of the Daughters of Compassion a few months later.'

'Not a nursing Order?'

'I thought of that, but it wouldn't have been fitting,' she said sadly. 'I had fallen asleep, you see. If I had remained awake Mrs. Carson might not have died. That much of the blame, at least, was mine. I told Mother Anne — she was Prioress then — the full story, of course. Mother Catherine was Novice Mistress when I entered and she also had to know. But nobody else in the Community was ever told, and I had no family. I was given the position of infirmarian as soon as I had made my final vows. That was a measure of Mother Catherine's confidence in me.'

'Surely it was justified!' I exclaimed.

'I was happy,' said Sister Felicity. 'Then Sister Eulalia came. She was younger than I am, only recently professed, but she'd helped her father write his memoirs and she'd seen a photograph of me. A hundred other people might have seen the picture and forgotten it, but not Sister Eulalia; not Enid Fox with her trained memory.'

'She didn't say anything to the others?'

Sister Felicity shook her head. 'But she let me know that she'd recognized me, with the verse, you see.'

'Sister Eulalia sounds perfectly horrid!' I exclaimed indignantly.

'Sister Eulalia was a little — spiteful at

times,' Sister Felicity conceded reluctantly. 'But we all have our faults, I suppose. And she's dead now, poor soul.'

'Of pneumonia,' I said.

Sister Felicity turned a haggard face towards me, her fingers pleating the serge of her habit.

'It was a cold,' she said miserably. 'Sister Eulalia caught a feverish cold and was moved to the guest house, to avoid the spread of infection. But she was not seriously ill and I took good care of her, better care than I would have taken of myself. But the cold grew suddenly worse, overnight. There was a fire in her room and she had plenty of covers on the bed. But when I brought her tea in the morning she was tossing and turning in a high fever. She died before the doctor came. But I didn't neglect her. I am a nurse, and my duty is to my patients.'

'Mother Catherine must have accepted that. You're still infirmarian, aren't you?'

She nodded, trying to look more cheerful.

'I pray for Sister Eulalia every day of my life,' she said softly.

'I know. I saw you in the chapel as I was coming across for my supper,' I said.

'In the chapel?' She gave me a puzzled look. 'When was this?'

'Half an hour ago, maybe a little longer.

The door was slightly ajar and I looked in and saw you praying before the altar.'

'But I haven't been to the chapel since supper. I came in here to wash up some of the dishes and to cut some fresh bread and butter. Sister Elizabeth reminded me that you had had no supper. It must have been one of the other Sisters you saw.'

'They had already left. It wasn't one of the others.'

'But I am the only — it must have been Sister Paul! The child has come back, and is in trouble of some kind.'

Sister Felicity was already at the kitchen door and I hurried at her heels through the refectory and the recreation rooms. The chapel was empty, the candles dripping wax.

'Sister Bridget had forgotten to snuff the candles,' Sister Felicity said.

'And Sister Paul doesn't seem to be here. But I did see a nun. I *did*!'

'She may have gone to her cell. I'll take a look. Would you be kind enough to look in the parlour?'

I went at once across the dark hall to the parlour. The fire had burned lower and there was a chill creeping into the room; or it might have been the cold spreading through me.

I went out into the hall again and stood, undecided. I had seen a nun in the chapel, had assumed it was Sister Felicity. Sister Paul was shorter and plumper. I didn't think I could have mistaken one for the other.

I wished some of the others would return. *Minstrel's Leap* echoed around me and the shadows flickered and danced round the walls.

I held my breath, listening to the beating of the rain against the windows and the sighing of the wind about the rafters. My skirt whispered over the floor as I went slowly to the gallery and stood looking up. Nothing moved beyond the low rail but the paler rectangles of windows were like eyes watching me.

I turned and walked swiftly to the nuns' quarters again. The impression that some-body watched my progress was so strong that I almost turned my head to check.

I was within the ante-room and Sister Felicity was hurrying towards me, shaking her head, when a dull thud sounded from the hall. For a moment we both stood perfectly still, gazing at each other. Then we were running into the hall, running and stopping, clutching at each other like two frightened children, and seeing, huddled below the gallery, the black shape of the little nun.

12

I felt a scream bubbling in my throat, and drove my teeth into my lower lip to keep myself silent. Sister Felicity drew in her breath with a hiss and then went over to kneel by the motionless figure.

Through a haze of shock I noticed that she was behaving instinctively like a nurse, lifting the limp wrist, bending to listen for a heart beat. Finally she stood up again and made the sign of the cross very carefully and reverently, before she came back to me.

'If you will ring the alarm bell in the guest house the noise may attract some attention and bring some of the Sisters back,' she said. 'I will stay here with Sister Paul.'

I nodded and went swiftly to the parlour to snatch up the lamp still burning on the table. At that moment I needed the comfort of light.

I came out into the hall again and turned to the guest house door. It opened at once and I recalled vaguely having left it unlocked hours before, so many hours before that I had lost all sense of time.

The rope for the bell hung in my bedroom

where Sister Felicity had shown it to me on my first day. As I went up the narrow stairs the flame of the lantern danced ahead of me on the walls. I entered my room and tugged the rope, relaxing as it clanged out urgently. Somebody would surely hear it.

When the strident echoes had died away I took up the lamp and went downstairs again. There was a shrinking reluctance in me to return to that huddled figure on the stone-flagged floor, but neither could I endure to remain alone in the guest house.

Sister Paul had been covered by a large tablecloth and Sister Felicity stood by the front door peering out.

'I got a cloth from the refectory to cover her decently,' she said as I joined her. 'Somebody will be here soon.'

'Someone is here.'

My ears had picked up the thudding of hooves across the turf. Sister Felicity held her own lantern higher and leaned out as the tall, cloaked figure on the horse swerved nearer.

'One of the Sisters has had an accident.'

More undisciplined than my companion I ran out and seized the animal's bridle as the rider paused.

'Are you from the village?'

But he was not from the village. As he stared down at me I recognized at once the dark features of the man who had sat opposite me in the train. I had sketched the man, had noticed his ugly hands and coat of foreign style.

'Mademoiselle?' His voice was harsh, grating upon my ear.

'One of the Sisters has had an accident.'

'Not Denise? It is not a Sister Denise who has suffered a mishap?'

'Sister Paul, one of the novices.'

'I heard the bell,' he frowned.

'The alarm bell. I rang it. Please, can you get some help?'

'You are certain that it is not a Denise?'

'Sister Paul. I told you. Sister Paul.'

'In that event, mademoiselle, it is none of my business.'

To my dismayed surprise, he wrested the bridle from my fingers and, setting spurs to the horse, rode away.

'Who was that?' Sister Felicity called.

'A stranger. He didn't — '

I broke off, seeing pinpoints of light advancing towards me.

'It's Mother Catherine and Sister Marguerite,' Sister Felicity exclaimed, 'and here are some of the others.'

I stood aside, shaking my head as they hurried past with brief, enquiring looks. It was not my place to break the news, nor to be there as an intrusion on their grief. So I pressed myself against the wet stone, listening to the low, shocked voices within the open door, watching the black-garbed women as they hurried to answer the summons of the bell.

'Verona, love! What are you doing out here?'

I had not heard him approach, but he was there, his arm about my shoulders, and something inside me cracked and broke so that I huddled within the shelter of his arm and sobbed bitterly.

'Sister Paul is dead. We found her — Sister Felicity and I found her.'

He gave me a startled look and ran up the steps into the hall. I heard his voice, quick and authoritative, and then he ran out again to me.

'I am going for the priest and the doctor. Go and change that wet gown and then make about a gallon of hot soup or tea; the Sisters will need it.'

He gave me a hard, comforting kiss and was gone again.

Inside every lantern blazed and every door stood open. The nuns were moving about aimlessly, water dripping from their habits, their voices low and shocked. Violent death had intruded twice into their peaceful lives and at that moment they were completely stunned. Mother Marie was weeping, her strong face crumpled like a child's.

'Sister Paul would never have disobeyed the rules so blatantly. She would never have done such a thing!' she repeated over and over.

'Sister Damian.' I touched the dark-eyed Sister on the arm and she turned a colour-drained face towards me. 'Will you come up to my room, Sister, and help me to get out of my wet things?'

She came at once, moving like a sleep-walker with eyes wide open. When we had reached my room she stood with her hands hanging limply and made not the slightest effort to assist me. My dress was wringing wet, the coils of hair drooping over my ears, my feet freezing.

'Sister Damian, your name is really Denise, isn't it?'

I was too upset to approach the subject tactfully.

Her face went, if it were possible, even whiter, and she swayed slightly.

'There was a gentleman out on the moor tonight. He asked me about you.' I hardened my heart against her stricken, beseeching look. 'I had seen him before. He was seated in the train opposite me when I was on my way north. I sketched him. That was what frightened you, wasn't it? The day you looked through my drawings you saw the one of the Frenchman.'

'What is it that you want?' she said at last. 'I haven't any money. Is it power over me that you want — as Sister Eulalia did? The power to sneer and hint that you could tell everybody what you knew if you cared to do it? Is that what you want?'

'Who is he, Sister? Who is the man?'

I pulled a dry gown over my head and began to take the pins out of my hair.

'He is my half-brother,' she said, but some of the dull apathetic air had gone from her bearing and her voice was puzzled.

'I know nothing of him or of your story,' I said gently. 'I saw him and sketched him by chance, but it's obvious you are in some great trouble.'

'Such trouble that I don't know what to do,' she said.

'Surely Mother Catherine — '

'No!' Her beautiful eyes flashed suddenly. 'I love Mother Catherine dearly. She is a very great woman and a fine Prioress, but I could never tell her.'

'About your half-brother?'

'My mother was married first to a Frenchman,' she said. 'But he was a bad man and a cruel husband. He was killed in a bar-room fight and my mother was left with a little boy to support. It was hard for a young widow with no family. She took in sewing for a time and she sang — she had a pretty voice — sang in bars and cafés. She was not a wicked woman, only weak and rather silly.'

'But she married again?' I prompted.

'She met a gentleman,' she said trem-blingly. 'An Englishman, much younger than she was, doing the European tour with his tutor. Claud, her son, was twelve years old. She didn't marry the Englishman. He returned with his tutor and I doubt if he ever knew that he had a daughter. My mother died when I was small, and my half-brother cared for me.'

'In France?'

'In Paris.' She nodded and sat down as if under the burden of Sister Paul's death her own reticence had been destroyed. 'We spoke English together, my brother and I. He was like my father, I think — cruel and greedy. He was pleased when he discovered that I had a nice singing voice. He took me round the cafés, to sing and dance for the customers. And when I was sixteen he told me that he had found a — a protector for me. An elderly man, dried and wrinkled like a prune with eyes like a lizard. But the man was rich, and would give me enough money.'

'To keep your brother in comfort?'

She nodded miserably and her dark eyes filled with tears.

'I took some of the money I had earned from my singing and dancing and I came to England. But I couldn't get work. All I knew was how to sing and dance; I hated doing that. I hoped to be a governess, but that was no use, for I had no references and very little education. In the end I took a job as a kitchen-maid in a big hotel. Some of the other girls used to help at a mission on their day off. It was a kind of soup centre, run by some nuns. They were so happy, so serene. I went to see the Mother Superior and asked her if she knew of any Order where they might take an untalented girl without a dowry. She laughed and said I sounded like an ideal recruit for the Daughters of Compassion.'

'But you didn't tell them about yourself?'

'I couldn't,' she said hopelessly. 'I was baptised Catholic but I hadn't practised my faith for years, and I had been born out of wedlock. I doubt if I'd even have been considered for the novitiate. So I spun them a tale of having been left an orphan and eventually I took my vows. I meant to tell

Mother Catherine one day, but I never could.'

'Sister Eulalia knew.'

'Her father had been a journalist and had taken her all over Europe with him when she was a very young girl. She had seen me several times singing and dancing, and she never forgot a face. She told me that and laughed about it. After she died I thought then I was safe.'

'And then I came.'

'With a sketch of my half-brother and some story of having been friendly with Sister Hyacinth. And now you say Claud is here, looking for me?'

I nodded.

'He must have tracked me down,' she said at last. 'Seven years since I ran away from him, and he finally reaches me. He will make me go back. If I refuse he will tell Mother Catherine about me and she isn't likely to keep a nun who has based her life upon a lie. And I was happy here.'

'You ought to tell the Prioress,' I urged. 'If she loves her nuns she will surely understand.'

'I can't tell her now, not now that Sister Paul is dead. It would only add to her troubles.'

'But later! You will tell her later?'

She nodded and rose, holding open the door for me.

'I knew Claud was in the district,' she said. 'We met Edith while we were out searching for Sister Paul, and she began chattering about a French gentleman who called at their house last night.'

'Edith was out, in the rain?'

'She often evades her cousin and wanders off by herself,' Sister Damian said. 'I told her to go home at once before she caught her death of cold.'

'And Sister Paul died,' I said slowly, and remembered Simon's words.

My little sister is as strong as a horse.

Frail-seeming, childishly petulant, or a ruthless and cunning murderess with a twisted hatred of anybody who stood in her way?

'Did Sister Eulalia get on with Edith?' I asked.

'Sister Eulalia didn't get on with anybody very well,' Sister Damian said. 'She may have teased Edith, said something hurtful — but why do you ask?'

I didn't know why I had asked. I wasn't sure of anything any more, except that in some way I wanted to protect Simon from the pain of knowledge.

The hall, formerly hushed and shadowy,

seemed in comparison crowded and noisy. All the searchers had apparently returned and there were several men in leather breeches and greatcoats. One of them, evidently a doctor, knelt by the now uncovered form, and Sister Elizabeth was hurrying about with mugs of tea. I recalled guiltily that I had been supposed to help her.

'Would you come into the parlour, Verona?'

Mother Marie, her eyes red-rimmed, came towards me.

'Yes, of course.'

I cast a look at the group round Sister Paul and went with the Novice Mistress to the parlour. Mother Catherine was there, her face grave and still, her expression disciplined into a quiet and uncomplaining grief.

'You have had a terrible day,' she said, sympathy in her handclasp. 'This second tragedy must have brought back the memory of your friend's death very vividly. But there is a question I must ask you.'

'Of course.'

I took the seat she indicated and tried to look calm and businesslike.

'Sister Felicity says that you saw one of the Sisters in the chapel.'

'Just a few minutes after you had all left,' I agreed. 'It was on my way to the refectory, and I passed the chapel. The door was ajar, and I glanced in. I assumed it was Sister Felicity and went through to have my meal without disturbing her.'

'She had her back to you?'

'She was kneeling with her hands over her face and her back to me. It looked like Sister Felicity, or perhaps I simply thought it was her because she was the only one left behind.'

'And as Sister Felicity had been in the kitchen, then the figure you saw must have been someone else.'

'None of the Sisters returned until the alarm bell sounded,' said Mother Marie, 'but Sister Paul must have been inside the house for a considerable time.'

'Her habit was dry and there was no mud on her shoes,' said Mother Catherine.

'Then she must have come back before it started to rain. But it didn't look like Sister Paul kneeling in the chapel,' I asserted.

'It could not have been Sister Paul whom you saw in the chapel,' said Mother Marie. 'Sister Felicity is severely shocked and Mother Catherine has sent her to bed, but she is a trained nurse.'

She paused, glancing at the Prioress.

'Sister Felicity felt for a pulse or for a heartbeat. She says there was nothing but she noted that Sister Paul's body was cold. Very cold, she said.'

'You mean — ?' I hesitated, glancing between them.

'When the doctor arrived I asked him if he could tell me how long Sister Paul had been dead,' said Mother Catherine. 'He said it was very hard to be accurate, but she had certainly been dead for at least eight hours.'

'Dead people cannot jump from galleries,' Mother Marie said harshly. 'Sister Paul was thrown down into the hall.'

'Her skull was fractured,' said Mother Catherine painfully.

'She was killed,' said Mother Marie. 'Somebody killed her, and that makes it probable that somebody killed Sister Hyacinth too.'

'It is assuming the proportions of a nightmare,' Mother Catherine said wearily. 'Nothing has gone well for us since our convent at York was burned down. Sister Eulalia's death, the guest house failing to pay — these things mount up, until one forgets the good things that have happened.'

'You will have to call in the Constable,' Mother Marie said.

'With all the attendant unpleasantness, questions, suspicions,' said the Prioress. 'I've read about these things, but I never imagined that they would ever touch this Community directly.'

I was not surprised that Sister Felicity had been ordered to bed, suffering from shock. The knowledge that she would have to undergo all the questioning again, that her past would have to be revealed — all that must have been an agony for her to anticipate.

'Simon will be back soon with Father,' said Mother Marie. 'He will advise us what to do. There has been so much coming and going this evening that there has scarcely been time to mourn. But Sister Paul will be most sadly missed. She was a promising young woman with a genuine vocation.'

'Her family will have to be informed,' said the Prioress. 'They live in Derbyshire; farmers. Sister Paul was one of several children, so we must prepare the guest house.'

'If you need my room — ' I began.

'We have ample accommodation without that,' said Mother Catherine swiftly. 'Now I am going to take advantage of my age and authority, and request you to go to bed. You are looking as shocked and upset as Sister Felicity, and you have already done more than your share in helping us.'

It was a gracious but firm dismissal. I returned her slight bow and went into the hall. People were drifting out through the front door and from the direction of the chapel came the sound of chanting.

I went back into the guest house and up the stairs to my room. I doubted if I would sleep very much that night. I was certainly tired, but my nerves were stretched so tightly that I could feel myself twitching at every creak of the wainscoting.

The wet dress I had taken off lay across the bed. I stretched out my hand to pick it up, and picked up instead a trailing black habit of coarse serge. The white coif and veil lying beneath it slithered to the floor.

I held the habit closer to examine it, but it told me nothing save that it was dry and clean, unspotted by mud or rain. And a few minutes before somebody had discarded it and tossed it on my bed.

13

My sleep was as disturbed as I had feared, for I tossed and turned most of the night, dreaming of nuns who flew like bats about the rafters and cried in Edith's high, sweet voice.

I may look frail but I am strong; strong; strong!

Sister Joan, the elderly assistant infirmarian, brought up my breakfast. I was touched that they had even remembered me, but when I got down in the hall I saw that an attempt had already been made to get back to normal.

The other novice, Sister Anne, was on her hands and knees scrubbing the floor clean of the previous night's dirt. She gave me a subdued good morning and returned to her task.

As I paused, the door to the parlour opened and Simon came out with a burly, blue-uniformed figure at his heels. He looked as tired as I felt, but his smile broadened as he caught sight of me.

'The Constable is anxious to have a word with you,' he said without preamble. 'I'll wait for you.'

By Constable I assumed he meant not the uniformed man, who now took up his position at the foot of the gallery steps, but the frock-coated gentleman whom I glimpsed sitting at the table in the parlour. Mother Catherine and also Mother Marie were there, and another policeman sat in the corner with an open notebook and a pencil.

'Please sit down,' Mother Catherine said. Her voice was calm and reassuring, with a slight edge of added authority, more for the policeman's benefit than mine, I suspected. To the gentleman in the frock coat she said, 'Miss Verona Dean was a friend of Sister Hyacinth's, as I told you. She came up to stay with us after hearing of Sister Hyacinth's death.'

The Constable gave me a little bow and began to question me. I answered briefly and truthfully, noting with gratitude that the questions were simple and uncomplicated, and not designed to trip me up. I said nothing about the habit I had found. It hung now in the wardrobe in my room, and would stay there until I had spoken to Mother Catherine about it.

'I think we have all the pertinent facts, Miss Dean,' he said at last. 'You will be staying for a while?'

'Yes, of course.'

'In that case I'll have a word with the Sisters now. We ought to be out of your way, Reverend Mother, by lunchtime.'

I went out into the hall again, past the stolid policeman, to the sweep of lawn sloping up to the open moor. Simon was standing there, his face intent and serious.

'Did they give you a bad time?' he asked as I joined him.

I shook my head and impulsively linked my hand through his arm.

'They were very polite.'

'And completely baffled,' he said with a faint smile. 'Most murders have a motive but who would want to kill an inoffensive young novice? It makes no sense.'

'And Sister Hyacinth? You don't believe that she fell accidentally from the gallery, do you?'

'It would be stretching coincidence rather too far, wouldn't it?' he commented.

'Then there was a connection between the two,' I said.

'If there was then the police will find it,' he said.

I wondered if I was expected to construe that as a warning not to meddle lest I uncover some secret that already nagged at him. And then I was ashamed to think that I could suspect him of ignoring murder in order to shield his own sister.

As if he sensed what was passing in my mind he said, 'Edith is very upset today, so Cousin Laura is keeping her in bed. We didn't tell her that it was anything except a very sad accident, but she will have to know sooner or later.'

'She was on the moors last night,' I could not resist saying.

'I know. Cousin Laura dozed off by the fire and Edith slipped out. She was in bed again by the time I got home. Cousin Laura was soaked to the skin. She woke up and went out to look for Edith.'

'It must have been a worry.'

'With strange foreigners in the district; yes.' He gave me a wry smile. 'I intended to talk about our wedding but it doesn't seem to be quite the time.'

'Who said it would ever be the time?' I challenged.

'Is there any reason why the subject should ever be completely banned?' he countered.

'One day — perhaps — ' I said vaguely, and that was unfair of me for he swung me round in delight and kissed me under the interested gaze of the policeman who had just emerged through the front door.

'I forgot to tell you. Laura has asked me to ask you to postpone our dinner tonight. With

Edith in bed, and nobody to do the cooking — '

'Yes, of course. We'll make it another time.'

A pang of disappointment shot through me, and I chided myself for allowing my desire to get the better of my discretion.

'The Constable will make his enquiries and then leave the convent in peace,' Simon told me. 'I thought it might be advisable for a man to be stationed outside but Mother Catherine doesn't agree. I believe she considers he would lower the dignity of the place.'

We were interrupted by Sister Damian who came around the side of the building and gave me the nervous, fleeting smile which indicated she wished to speak to me.

I moved away from Simon towards her, and she said, with a gallant attempt at cheerfulness, 'I have to go in and see the Constable now. But I will ask Mother Catherine if I may speak to her privately. It is time that I told her.'

'I admire your courage,' I said, but envy would have been a more accurate word.

'I don't think I have very much of it,' she said forlornly, and squared her shoulders as she went into the house.

'I'd like to take you somewhere for the entire day,' Simon said when I rejoined him, 'but I promised to bring up supplies and let the school know that Sister Bridget and Sister Marguerite won't be in for a couple of days. You can come with me if you like.'

I did like but some instinct bade me shake my head. The feeling that some part of me retained the answer to the riddle of Sister Paul's death and the deaths of Sister Eulalia and Sister Hyacinth bound me to *Minstrel's Leap*.

'I'll see you tomorrow morning,' I promised, and wondered guiltily if it were very wrong of me to hope for one more meeting before I was driven to confess my past.

I would move my easel and canvas from the church until after the funeral, I decided. Within a day or so Sister Paul's relatives would be arriving. I watched Simon until he was out of sight and then I went back into the house and turned towards the chapel.

Candles burned now on the altar and at the four corners of the bier on which Sister Paul had been laid. Two of the nuns knelt in prayer by the body. I guessed a vigil would be kept there until she was buried.

I knelt to pay my own respects, uneasy in the presence of death, repelled by the chill, sweet smell that reminded me of the cold, stone slab on which my father had been laid. There had been the same perfume of death then, and the loneliness of knowing that

Pierre would never marry me now, would never marry the daughter of a suicide.

I rose from my knees and went over to the canvas and felt a sickness rise in me. I had painted in a shadowy background of brown and grey touched faintly with yellow and sketched a vague outline of the altar. But that was smeared beyond repair now and in white paint, daubed thickly, a figure capered. A stick figure with arms and legs thin as antennae and a round leering face framed in some kind of veil.

I turned the canvas to the wall and anger rose up in me at this act of spiteful and childish obscenity.

'Verona.' Sister Damian's whisper reached me from the door.

'What is it, Sister?'

I went out into the hall, but her shining eyes gave me the answer to the question even before she spoke.

'I told Mother Catherine about myself. It's going to be all right. She says that no matter what my beginnings I have earned my place in the Community. She is going to send to the village to find out where Claud is staying. The police will want to question him anyway, and then Mother Catherine says that she and I will face him together.'

Remembering the Prioress's icy bearing

when she was displeased, I could almost feel sorry for the coarse-fingered Claud.

'It is rather selfish of me to be so happy, with Sister Paul lying there,' Sister Damian breathed, 'but I feel as if somebody had lifted a heavy weight from my shoulders and I was free!'

'It's not selfish, and I'm happy for you,' I said.

'If only I had been completely frank from the beginning I could have saved myself so much heartache,' she confided. 'Now I can stay here with my Sisters and take care of the garden. I have so many ideas for bringing new plants up to this area and seeing if they will grow. And that reminds me — I want to make a wreath for Sister Paul. She loved those feathery strands of white and purple heather.'

'Would you like me to come with you?'

'It's very kind of you,' she said, 'but Mother Marie asked me to take Sister Anne. We're going to tidy up the other graves and put some flowers on them, before the funeral. We want to have everything as nice as possible for Sister Paul's relatives.'

I turned back to the chapel, and picked up the mutilated painting, carrying it swiftly across the hall to the door of the guest house. The nuns were upset enough already, and the sight of that picture would cause them even more pain. I stayed in my room only long enough to push the canvas under the bed and to check that the habit was still in the wardrobe and then, uneasy with my own company, I went downstairs again and through to the kitchen.

Sister Elizabeth was there, scouring the pans as if sheer energy could dispel grief. When I offered to help her she gave me a swift look and then handed me a tea-towel with no word of protest. By her action she made me part of the Community, no longer merely a visitor, and I thought her gesture both delicate and kindly.

Dinner was a silent meal, for the period of mourning had begun and there was no reading to distract the mind. After the meal the Sisters went to their cells, two of them going to the chapel to replace the two who came now for a late meal.

I went into the kitchen to help with the washing up and was not prevented, but after a while the feeling that Sister Elizabeth wanted to be alone in order to enjoy the luxury of a hearty weep drove me out to the moors again.

They were serene and beautiful as if the rain and wind of the previous night had never been. I had my sketch book as usual, and though it was still too damp to risk sitting on the grass I did manage to capture some essence of the waving grass, shading into purple as I followed it with my eyes towards the belt of trees surrounding the little cemetery.

The shadows of the trees were long and thin under the pale sunlight when I turned back towards *Minstrel's Leap*. The graciousness of its façade struck me again as I walked across the gently sloping lawn.

The Constable and his two satellites had gone, and it was hard to imagine that death — violent death — had struck twice in the past months. But why? It was madness to believe that these quiet women leading their inoffensive lives could have inspired such hatred in the mind of one person that she could kill and kill again. But poor Edith was not normal. Her mind had been arrested, but did arrested mean twisted?

I went in for supper, wishing that Simon were coming for me to drive me over to his house. I would have endured Edith's petulance and Cousin Laura's fussy kindness for the sake of being with him for a few hours.

The Prioress drew me aside as we filed out.

'Sister Damian tells me that you know her history,' she said.

'Only what she told me.'

'She was very foolish not to have told me at the beginning, but Mother Marie and I were even more to blame for not divining her trouble, for not winning her confidence sufficiently. But that is in the past.'

'And her brother?' I asked.

'He has been questioned by the police for several hours already,' said Mother Catherine. 'Sister Damian's brother — half-brother I should say — has led a rather shady existence, I suspect, and is not at all anxious to have the attention of the police drawn to him. And if the Constable cannot persuade him to leave, then *I* am quite ready to interview him.'

I didn't doubt it, and was more than ever convinced that Claud of the ugly hands would be well advised to make speedy tracks for Paris, and stay there.

'Simon is going over to Derbyshire tomorrow to see some of Sister Paul's relatives,' Mother Catherine said. 'Edith was apparently very upset by Sister Paul's death. The child is very attached to us, as we are to her. Indeed I have made it quite clear to the Shaws that if Simon ever thinks of taking a wife, we would be very happy to accept Edith as a lay-Sister here. Our Rule makes provision for that if the Prioress of any convent deems it necessary.'

I opened my mouth and closed it again, helpless in the face of her innocent charity. She was qualified to deal with a cheap scoundrel like the Frenchman, but how could she possibly be expected to cope with a twisted and dangerous maniac?

There was no recreation because of the mourning, so I went up to the guest house at once and sat for a long time in the lower sitting-room reading a book. To be more precise, I sat with a book in my hands, letting my eyes rove over the pages, while my ears were strained for some sound that I knew I would recognize.

It came at last, just after my fob-watch had displayed the hour of ten. The nuns would be asleep now, save for the two in the chapel, but the footsteps creeping up to my bedroom were light and quick and feminine. I waited for a few minutes with hammering heart, and then I closed the book, and took the lamp, and followed softly up the stairs.

Edith was standing by the wardrobe, the black habit in her hands. She turned as I came in and gave me the blank, bright stare of a person jerked into awareness. Then her exquisite doll face broke into a pleased smile.

'Why didn't you tell me that you had Cousin Laura's habit here?'

'Cousin Laura's,' I echoed.

'When she was a girl, before she got married, she was a nun for a time. Not a real nun, but a novice. She left and got married though.'

'Cousin Laura was a nun?'

'Years and years ago, when she was in her teens. I found the habit once when I was playing in the attic above the chapel. Cousin Laura was very angry and took it away from me. I haven't seen it since then.'

It fell into place as if I had clicked home the last piece of a jigsaw. The fire at York, the deaths of the three nuns, the failure of the guest house — it was almost all clear now.

I knew it as I stared back at Edith, hearing her say, 'The habit is mine, isn't it? Now that I've run away to live with the Sisters.'

14

'Run away?' I echoed stupidly

Edith was already pulling the habit over her head but emerged from its folds to giggle.

'I left a note, telling them I was coming to take Sister Paul's place. Cousin Laura will be here soon, won't she?'

I was certain that Cousin Laura would be here soon, and the hammering of my heart increased in volume and pace.

'Where is Simon tonight?' I asked sharply.

'He went to have dinner with the Constable. He won't be back for ages and ages. Anyway Simon won't mind at all. Why should he? He never scolds me or tries to keep me away from the nuns.'

'Edith, if you're to stay here we will have to tell Mother Catherine,' I said.

'They'll be asleep now.'

'Not the nuns in the chapel. We can tell one of them that you're here if you like.'

'They will let me pray with them,' Edith said happily.

'Then we'll go down now.'

I took her hand and drew her out of the room and down the corridor to the stairs. She came docilely, the coifed veil in her other hand, her red hair floating over the high neck of the black gown.

The great hall was shadowed and silent, every door closed. The lamp I still carried made a pool of radiance about us.

Edith had stopped suddenly, her face raised up to the gallery. I followed her gaze and my heart stopped hammering and slowed down, and my hands were icy.

'The minstrel has come,' Edith whispered. 'But he's too late, isn't he, Verona? Because I'm wearing the wrong dress.'

Before I could prevent her she had run past me to stand below the gallery and her voice floated up sweetly to that dark figure outlined against the window panes.

'You're too late! You must go away because I am one of the Sisters now.'

The dark figure came to the rail and Cousin Laura said, 'You mustn't talk like that, Edith. You don't understand what it means, child. You don't know these women as I know them. They bring death and pain and loss.'

'As they did to you?' I went to stand beside Edith.

'They took my mother first,' said Cousin Laura. 'I was very small and they sent me away on a holiday because my mother was ill.

And when I came back there was a nun there. I heard them say she was a nun, and she took my hand and went with me into my mother's bedroom and lifted me up. And my mother was in a long box, with flowers in her hands, and her face was cold, cold as wax and white, like a candle.'

'Who took care of you then?'

I had moved to the foot of the gallery stairs.

'My sister, Jane, took care of me,' she said. 'She was nineteen and very beautiful and gentle. She said 'I will be your mother now'; and she was, for six long years.'

'What happened to Jane?'

I put my foot cautiously on the bottom step.

'She went away for a long time,' said Cousin Laura. 'My uncle looked after me and he was very kind, but he wasn't Jane. Jane laughed a lot and she had lovely red hair.'

'Did you see her again?'

'Once. In a big church, with her in white and a bridal wreath on her head. We were all there and the choir was singing. And then she came back in a black dress with her hair cut short. She went beneath an iron grille in the wall and she never looked at me. The grille clanged down behind her and the choir sang louder and louder. And she never looked at me.'

'And you never saw her again?'

'She died,' said Cousin Laura. 'They killed her, you see, behind the grille and the stone walls. Sometimes I used to dream she was not dead, only waiting.'

'So you became a nun?'

'To find Jane again,' she nodded, 'but they said I had no vocation, and wouldn't let me make my final vows. It was a plot to stop me from discovering how Jane had died. They let me keep my habit when I came home again.'

'To be married?'

I was inching my way up the stairs.

'He was a kind man and we were happy,' she said. 'I never had any babies of my own, but there were my cousin's children — Simon and Edith. After my husband died I reared Edith and she was Jane made little for me to love.'

'Until the train crash.'

'My cousin died. A good man and a friend, and he died. I went to York at once — Simon and I went. Edith was very ill but they wouldn't let me take care of her. The nuns would look after her, they said, and you see how it is. They did something to her, stopped her mind from growing, wheedled her into loving them more than she loved me. Oh, they were very clever! but I was cleverer than they were.'

'You burned down the convent.'

The great door behind me had opened and I heard footsteps advance and pause. I was too wary to turn my head, but kept my eyes on Cousin Laura. She was talking more rapidly now, the words spilling out, her face and hands white against the black jerkin and tights.

'Simon offered them *Minstrel's Leap* and we lived in Shaw Cottage. Edith's home and my home, given to those black crows! Oh, I said nothing! What would have been the point of it? Simon and Edith thought the nuns could do no wrong. They didn't know about my mother and Jane, you see. So I had to move very carefully, to bide my time.'

'You had keys to the house.'

I was on the gallery now, level with her.

'I had keys,' she said triumphantly, 'and I had infinite patience. I found this suit up in the attic over the chapel. It had been made for a fancy dress ball years ago, and my old habit too. I wore them.'

'To frighten guests away from the guest house?'

'Through the sliding panel at the back of the wardrobe. I frightened you, didn't I, on the first night?'

'And Sister Eulalia?'

'She had a very bad cold, and her bed was near the window. I mixed her a double dose of laudanum and came up when Sister Felicity had gone to bed. She was pleased to see me, was Sister Eulalia, but then I was always in and out, helping the nuns. She slept heavily, and I opened the windows wide and stripped off the bedclothes. I didn't mean her to die. I meant to make her suffer a little, but not to die. I closed the window and covered her up, you know, before I left. But she died in spite of that.'

'And Sister Hyacinth?'

'That was an accident too,' she said earnestly. 'I wanted to frighten the nuns, that's all. I was up here in the minstrel's outfit, and she came through into the hall. I expected her to run screaming for the others, to give me time to get away, but she was disobedient. She came up the stairs to the gallery to see who it was. I took her by surprise, you see, but then I'm very strong, much stronger than I look.'

'And Sister Paul?'

'She was by herself, looking for birds in the trees; silly creature! I told her that I had seen an injured bird on the ground and she came with me and knelt down to part the grass, and I took up a stone, and hit her and hit her and hit her.'

'You met Simon and me.'

'I said I'd seen two nuns on their way to the graves with flowers. If they'd found Sister Paul there I had to put the blame on somebody, didn't I?'

'How did you get her back to the convent?'

'That was very difficult,' she said. 'I carried her. I could have said I'd just found her if I'd met anyone, I suppose, but I was most fortunate. I never met a single soul, and I brought her up to the gallery and laid her close to the wall under the window ledge. She couldn't be seen from below at all.'

'And nobody thought of looking for her there. That *was* clever of you.'

'I waited until it was darker and then I went to the attic and put on my habit. I'd worn it before, when I slipped among the nuns and put the doll on the altar, and slipped upstairs again while they were busy at their prayers. Nuns keep their eyes on the ground and don't often stare at one another.'

'And then when you had said your own prayers you threw Sister Paul over the rail.' Disgust thickened my voice.

'When you had gone to the guest house, I waited until Sister Felicity fetched a cover for the body, then I came down into the hall and into the guest house after you. I was hiding in

218

the lower room when you were ringing the alarm bell. I left the habit on your bed after you'd gone, and slipped out through the window downstairs.'

From the hall below us, Edith called up angrily.

'I woke up and you weren't in the house and I came to look for you. And when I found you on the moor you said *you* were looking for *me*! That was a lie, Cousin Laura. The Sisters don't tell lies.'

'They do, they do.'

She had turned to lean over the rail, and I, also turning, perceived the shapes below, moving silently.

'You're very sick,' I said loudly. 'You need a doctor.'

'Don't tell me what I need!' she snapped. 'Go back and paint the chapel. I helped with that painting, for I put the minstrel in the picture. Did you see him?'

'You're sick,' I said again.

'I shall be quite well as soon as Edith is better,' she said, with a dreadful kind of politeness in her voice. 'I have to take care of Edith. The nuns will hurt her. Look at them!'

'That's another lie!' Edith shouted from below. 'The nuns are kind and I'm going to stay with them for ever. I love them, and I hate you!'

'That's not true,' Cousin Laura cried. 'They will kill you and put you in a long box and you will be as cold as ice and as white as a candle!'

'Laura!'

I stretched out my hand, willing her to calmness, but she was past all persuasion. I doubt if she even heard me or was fully aware of her surroundings.

At that moment she saw only Edith and even as Simon called, 'Laura, for God's sake!' she had vaulted the low rail. For an instant she seemed almost to hover in the air, and then the black figure fell and the crack of its impact on the stone floor was almost drowned by Edith's shrill and frightened scream.

My knees sagged beneath me and the lamp in my hand shook as if I stood in a gale. Below, above the exclamations of horror and surprise, I could hear Simon's voice, carefully controlled.

I closed my eyes and leaned against the window, knowing that he would come for me. He came up in a very few minutes, and I clung to him while the words I had been ashamed to utter flowed out of me.

'I loved a man and I thought he meant to marry me. But my father was sick, drink-crazed, wasting his money and squandering his talents. That was his tragedy, he could not accept the truth; that he was not quite a genius. He couldn't live with that. So he set his studio on fire and cut his wrists and leaped from the window. And I ran and ran through the streets to find Pierre, but he closed the door in my face. He said he couldn't afford the scandal. He was of good family and he couldn't afford the scandal!'

'Not now, think of it later. Think of it later, calmly, as I will think of Laura,' he said. 'We will face these things together and then put them out of our minds and go on.'

'Together?'

'If that is what you want, love.'

'It is; it is,' I said, and felt his arms tightly around me and his cheek pressed against mine.

When we came down into the hall again we were swept up into the circle of black-garbed Sisters, many of them shocked out of sleep by Sister Joan, who had been disturbed by our voices in the hall and had come from the chapel to see.

'I returned early from the dinner, hoping to see you for a few minutes before you went to bed,' Simon said.

He was looking unbelievingly at the inert form spreadeagled on the stone. Mother Catherine was hurrying Edith away, and

221

Mother Marie was pulling on a cloak with the intention, I assumed, of seeking help.

'She was always so good to us,' she said in a low, troubled voice. 'She was always so kind.'

'And shall be remembered for that,' a voice said at our elbow. 'The poor lady was sick in the head. The grief of that will pass as the night passes. Come out to the front now, the pair of you and take a breath of air. The worst part is over.'

Across the black sky, stars hung low and the waving grass was silhouetted against the rising moon. I leaned within the circle of his arm and felt the sweet wind lift the hair from my brow.

'Glory be to God,' said Sister Bridget, 'but it's going to be a lovely day tomorrow.'

THE END

Other titles in the
Ulverscroft Large Print Series:

DEAD FISH

Ruth Carrington

Dr Geoffrey Quinn arrives home to find his children missing, the charred remains of his wife's body in the boiler and Chief Superintendent Manning waiting to arrest him for her murder. Alison Hope, attractive and determined, is briefed to defend him. Quinn claims he is innocent, but Alison is not so sure. The background becomes increasingly murky as she penetrates a wealthy and ruthless circle who cannot risk their secrets — sexual perversion, drugs, blackmail, illegal arms dealing and major fraud — coming to light. Can Alison unravel the mystery in time to save Quinn?